Jennifer's Secret

Cedar River Daydreams

Other Books by Judy Baer

Live! From Brentwood High

Jennifer's Secret

Judy Baer

BETHANY HOUSE PUBLISHERS
MINNEAPOLIS, MINNESOTA 55438
A Division of Bethany Fellowship, Inc.

Jennifer's Secret
Judy Baer

Library of Congress Catalog Card Number 88–63463

ISBN 1–55661–058–0

Published by Bethany House Publishers
A Division of Bethany Fellowship, Inc.
6820 Auto Club Road, Minneapolis, Minnesota 55438

Printed in the United States of America

For my daughter,
Jennifer Joy Baer,
With love.

JUDY BAER received a B.A. in English and Education from Concordia College in Moorhead, Minnesota. She has had fifteen novels published and is a member of the National Romance Writers of America, the Society of Children's Book Writers and the National Federation of Press Women.

Two of her novels have been prizewinning bestsellers in the Bethany House SPRINGFLOWER SERIES (for girls 12–15); *Adrienne* and *Paige*. Both books have been awarded first place for juvenile fiction in the National Federation of Press Women's communications contest.

Chapter One

Two days. Was it possible that was all that was left of summer vacation?

Lexi Leighton stretched her slender legs and tilted her head backward over the edge of the bed until her long hair swayed against the floor. Turning her head slightly, she listened to the chatter of the three girls on the other side of her bedroom.

Binky and Peggy were debating the merits of entering their sophomore year at Cedar River High.

"It's going to be great," Peggy Madison announced. "I'm signing up for Computer Club. That and girls' basketball should keep me totally involved this year. No more sitting on the sidelines!"

Lexi opened one eye and stared with disbelief at Peggy. Peggy's parents were avid travelers. She'd already been all over the United States. And now her family was discussing next summer's trip to England—that was hardly "sitting on the sidelines."

Binky McNaughton curled her scrawny knees to her chest and rested her chin on the shelf they made. Her gray-green eyes gazed thoughtfully out the window into the oncoming darkness. "I wish I could be like that," she said mournfully. "I think I'll be on the sidelines forever."

"Don't be such a dope," Jennifer Golden retorted grumpily as she added the final touches of pale pink nail polish to her toes. She'd stuck cotton balls between each toe to spread them apart. Her feet looked like little pink cotton plants ripe for harvest. "You get good grades. Teachers like you. Who cares if you're on the sidelines or not?"

All three girls looked at Jennifer in surprise, but she stared intently at her toes, not lifting her head to see what her comment had inspired.

Quietly, Binky murmured, "Good grades aren't everything, Jenna."

When Jennifer glanced upward, her eyes were cloudy and unreadable. "Oh, yeah. I keep forgetting." Then the sullen cloudiness was replaced with her familiar, cocky glint. "I'm on vacation. This school talk is boring." She wiggled her widespread toes in the air. "Booooorrrrring!"

Just then, Lexi's little brother burst into her room with an ear-splitting shout. " 'Cademy, here comes Ben!" The door bounced off the wall behind it and shuddered. At the same moment Lexi's poster of a tabby cat suspended from a branch and advising "Hang in there" slid to the floor, and the lamp shade on the nightstand tipped sideways.

"How does he *do* that?" Binky wondered in awe. "How can anyone that little make that much noise?"

Ben stood in the middle of the room smiling benignly and repeated, " 'Cademy, here comes Ben!" He clutched a small blue schoolbag from which protruded a pencil box and a gigantic box of crayons.

"What's going on, kid?" Jennifer inquired gruffly, seeming pleased by the interruption.

" 'Cademy starts."

"And what's that?" Jennifer leaned forward and stared directly into Ben's brown, almond-shaped eyes.

"You know. *'Cademy.*" He reached up and stroked her cheek with the knuckles of his right hand.

Jennifer glanced at Lexi. "Do you want to translate?"

Lexi slid to the edge of her bed. "He's talking about the new academy for the handicapped. My parents have enrolled him for this fall. Ben's excited about school."

"Good for you, tiger," Jennifer announced. Her voice wavered a bit as she spoke. "I'm proud of you."

Lexi stared at her friend throughout the exchange. Ben and Jennifer were fond of each other. That had come after their rocky start when Jennifer first learned that Ben had Down's syndrome. Since those early days she'd learned to love Ben almost as much as Lexi did herself. Still, that didn't account for the unhappy expression in Jennifer's eyes tonight.

As quickly as he'd entered, Ben spun around on the stubby toe of his tennis shoe and headed for the door. "Go now. 'Bye." He hoisted his pack to his shoulder and sauntered from the room with his distinctive rolling gait.

"He's so *cute,*" Binky said to no one in particular. "I've always felt that way about starting school in the fall." Her pale eyes began to sparkle. "I love the thought of new pencils and notebooks with every page untouched and new clothes and—"

"New teachers who don't know you like to chew gum in class—"

"Or haven't found out who your friends are and tried to separate you. Then you can always find seats together and talk when he's out of the room—"

"And new guys," Binky added dreamily. "There's always the chance that someone has moved to town during the summer and hasn't found out that I have a weird brother named Egg."

At that comment everyone broke into gales of laughter. Everyone, that is, but Jennifer.

Binky and Peggy continued their conversation, which had now meandered onto such topics as the merits of being chosen to sing with the high school's swing choir—The Emerald Tones—or being selected to be on the staff of the *Review*, the school's newspaper.

Lexi sat and watched Jennifer as she finished polishing her toenails and began methodically plucking the cotton from between her toes, dropping the wads into the garbage can. She was stiff and tense, like a spring coiled too tightly, and her movements were sharp and unnatural. A sullenness had overtaken her.

"Jenna?" Lexi began gently, "are you all right?"

"Of course I am," was the abrupt response. "What makes you think I'm not?"

Lexi shrugged her slim shoulders helplessly. "Nothing, I guess. You just don't seem very . . . happy."

"Why should I be? What's to be happy about?"

The venom in Jennifer's voice was startling. Lexi remembered Jennifer at the first musical rehearsal Lexi had attended. Jennifer had stood in the back row singing exuberantly, pretending to read from sheet music she'd turned upside down. That had been an entirely different person from the tense, unhappy girl who faced Lexi tonight.

"I thought you'd be trying out for the Emerald Tones, Jenna. If you get into the swing choir, you'll be going on tour and performing around Cedar River and—"

"*If*, I get in. That's the key word. If." Jennifer frowned. "Who says Mrs. Waverly will let me in? After all, I'm the one who dropped out of the summer musical when the Hi-Fives wanted me to."

"But you came back," Lexi pointed out logically, glad those tense times of her early days in Cedar River were over.

So much had happened since Lexi and her family had moved to Cedar River. She recalled her nasty encounter with the Hi-Fives; the revealing experiences with their leader, Minda Hannaford; Lexi's starring role in the summer musical; her brother's life-threatening accident; her job at Camp Courage, and, best of all, the friends she'd made—Todd Winston, Egg McNaughton, and the three crazies on the other side of her bedroom.

"Maybe." Jennifer flopped onto her stomach across the bed and stared out the window into the darkness split occasionally with a shaft of car headlights. "Maybe not. You don't understand."

"Then give me a chance," Lexi murmured softly, glancing to where Peggy and Binky were busy in front of the mirror experimenting with each other's hair. "Help me understand."

"You can't." Jennifer's tone was muffled.

"Try me," Lexi offered. "If I'm willing to make a stab at understanding Minda Hannaford, whatever *you* say should be simple. Right?"

Jennifer gave a weak smile. Everyone knew how difficult Minda could be—and how very cruel she'd been to Lexi. "It won't work, Lexi. There's nothing to understand."

"Then why are you acting so—"

Before Lexi could finish, Jennifer jumped to her feet and clapped her hands. "All right, guys, no more schlumping around! We got together for fun and we're going to have it! Music! Lights! Action!" And she twisted the volume dial on the radio as far as it would go and began to sing along at the top of her lungs, waving with her hands, encouraging Peggy and Binky to join in.

Lexi winced, wondering what her parents were thinking downstairs in the living room. Then she perched on the edge of the bed and stared at Jennifer. What was *wrong* with her tonight?

Lexi tucked her thoughts and observations into the back of her mind. *Later,* she thought, *later I'll find out just what's going on in that blond head of Jennifer's.*

It was five A.M. when Lexi ran into Binky in the kitchen of the Leighton home.

"What are you doing up?" Lexi wondered as Binky came wandering into the kitchen rubbing her eyes and yawning so widely it appeared her face would split.

The soft blue glow of the backlight on the stove and the first pink and orange rays of sunrise lit the room. Otherwise it was dark except for the small reading light Lexi was using.

"What are *you* doing? It's practically the middle of the night!" Binky retorted. She curled into the chair across from Lexi's and put her elbows on the table to cradle her chin in her hands.

"Reading. I couldn't sleep. Peggy snores."

"Yeah," Binky agreed. "She kept me awake too. I thought about stuffing a sock in her mouth, but I decided to get up and find a glass of milk instead."

Lexi smiled. "Refrigerator. Left-hand side. Bring me one too."

Willingly, Binky raided the cupboard for glasses and poured two tall glasses of milk. As she returned to the table to place one in front of Lexi, she asked, "What are you reading?"

"My Bible," Lexi murmured softly. "I like to read it early in the morning before the day starts. When it's quiet like this and the sun is just coming up it feels so . . ." she struggled for a word, "right."

Binky looked at her in amazement. There wasn't much attention paid to spiritual things at the McNaughton household.

"Sometimes it's hard to talk to God when there are people trying to talk to you." Lexi gave a shrug. "I guess it's just one of those conversations that you get more out of when it's One-to-one."

"Makes sense," Binky responded cheerfully. "Want me to leave?"

"No. I've been reading for a while already. It's all right."

"Whatcha reading in there?" Binky asked curiously. "As if *I'd* know what it was."

"I'm reading from the book of Mark in the New Testament," Lexi explained. Seeing the confusion on Binky's face, she continued. "The books of the Bible have many different authors. Some books are very short, like James, which is only a few pages, and others are quite long. All the books together make up the Bible."

"So what does Mark have to say today?" Binky asked. Her tiny features were intent and interested.

"Today I was reading about prayer." Lexi thumbed to the eleventh chapter. "It says that if you have faith in God, you can ask anything of Him and He will answer you."

"Wow." Binky's eyes were large and her face shadowed by the lengthening light of morning.

Lexi nodded. "I know. I like that. Sometimes when I feel like I've lost control of everything and begin to think life is pretty hopeless after all, I read that. It reminds me that I don't have to go through anything alone."

"But what if it's not . . . you know . . . true?"

Lexi smiled. "This is probably the most reliable book you're ever going to find, Binky. The more you study it, the more you realize that. And, anyway, having faith is what Christianity is all about. You just have to lean back and trust that God's Word *is* true."

Binky swirled the last drops of milk in the bottom of her glass. "Every time we talk you give me a lot to think about, Lexi. I've never known anyone quite like you before."

Lexi laughed. "That's great, isn't it? No two people quite alike? That makes every day an adventure!"

"Yeah," Binky agreed. "But some days are more of an adventure than I care for."

A frown flitted across Lexi's features as she laced her fingers together and leaned toward Binky. "Bink, what's wrong with Jennifer? She's so . . . touchy."

Binky shrugged. "Who knows? Ask her."

"I did. She won't give me an answer. I'm worried about her. She's changed so much in the past few days."

"Don't worry about it. You just aren't used to it, that's all."

"Used to what?"

"Jennifer's school mood."

"Her *school mood*? What does that mean?"

Binky moved to pour herself another glass of milk. "Every year at this time, Jennifer starts acting strange. Grumpy. Out-of-sorts. Cranky. She just hates school."

"Hate is a pretty strong word, Binky."

"Maybe, but I really think she does. Parts of it, at least."

"But why? Does she get bad grades?"

"I really don't know. She's not on the honor roll, but I've never heard that she gets anything but average grades. She'll get over it. Don't worry. Jennifer just likes being gloomy in the fall."

"She's this way *every* year?"

"Has been since I can remember."

Lexi stared thoughtfully into the bottom of her own glass as Binky padded to the refrigerator to return the milk carton to its place.

Gloomy? Was that really all it was?

Chapter Two

"Why so glum, Lexi? This is your first day of school in Cedar River!" Todd Winston said, as he met Lexi on the front porch of her house. "Nerves?"

"Sort of," she admitted. "My stomach has so many butterflies that it feels like it's two minutes to lift-off."

"You look great," Todd said admiringly. "You'll be fine once you get there. I'll show you the ropes."

Lexi smoothed a hand across her denim skirt. She'd worked very hard at her outfit this morning. She'd finished embroidering the pattern on the yoke of her shirt at midnight. It had been a lot of work to duplicate the beautiful hand-embroidered blouse she'd seen at the mall, but the effort was worth it. Her shirt could have come directly from a glass display window instead of off the arm of her sewing machine.

"Thanks," she murmured softly. "I just have so many things racing through my mind today." She still couldn't get the thought of Jennifer's strange behavior out of her head. Her complete about-face had shaken Lexi.

"Yeah, I know what you mean," Todd agreed. "I feel a little funny about going back to school today too."

"Oh?"

"I keep wondering about Jerry Randall—if he's going to be in class or . . . what."

They walked toward school in a thoughtful silence, both unaware of the thick green lawns and lush canopy of leaves overhead.

Jerry Randall was the first boy Lexi had met when she moved to Cedar River. He was handsome, charming, and a wonderful catch—or at least that's what she'd thought at first. It hadn't taken long to discover that Jerry had some *big* problems.

Those problems had all come to a head the night that he was unlawfully racing his car and hit Lexi's little brother Ben.

"Do you know what's been happening with him?"

Todd shrugged. "Not really. My brother Mike has been following his case. Mike would like to help Jerry—if he could." Todd smiled thoughtfully. "Mike's a great one for wanting to help people."

"Yeah, I know what you mean," Lexi murmured. She had someone in mind who seemed to need some help of her own right now, but Lexi didn't have one clue as to what she could do.

Thoughts of Jennifer and Jerry vanished from her mind as they approached the school. It was a honeycomb of activity—doors swinging, students mingling, and teachers occasionally glancing around as they considered trying to control the situation.

As they neared, Lexi could feel the excitement and sense of anticipation in the air. The halls smelled of fresh wax and cleaning compounds, and everything appeared newly painted and polished for the opening day.

The long gray lockers were already losing their nondescript sameness. Someone had hung a big pink bow on the handle of one locker, another displayed a small sign announcing "Sherry's Place." Lexi's home-room was nearly full. Todd left her at the door with a squeeze on the elbow. "I've got to go meet Coach Derek. Good luck and have fun."

Lexi took a deep breath, forced a smile to her face and stepped inside. The din subsided for a fraction of a second as everyone turned to study her. Lexi saw Peggy and Binky together near the far wall, their arms draped protectively over an empty desk.

"This is for you," Peggy mouthed. "Come here!"

Gratefully Lexi moved to the spot. It was a relief to sink into the seat and be away from the center of the room and all the eyes that had followed her.

"Thanks. I didn't realize I was so late."

"You aren't. Everybody else is early. I can't sleep late the first day of school—I suppose no one else can either." Binky glanced around the room before adding, "I wonder if Egg found Coach Derek."

"That's where Todd was headed too." Lexi glanced around the room. "Speaking of people finding one another, where's Jennifer?"

Peggy shrugged. "Who knows? She's probably going to be late. That girl has a death wish where school is concerned."

"What do you mean by that?"

Peggy glanced at Binky and her eyes shadowed. "You'll see for yourself pretty soon. Jennifer just . . . changes . . . when school starts." Peggy lowered her voice. "My mom is a good friend of a couple of the teachers. They don't like Jennifer very much. They call her a 'discipline problem.' "

"*Jennifer?*" Lexi could hardly believe it. Jennifer might act crazy and high-spirited once in a while, but everyone did. "I don't understand."

"You don't have to," Peggy concluded. "You'll see for yourself."

"She and Mrs. Waverly seem to get along."

"Sure," Peggy informed her. "There are a few teachers and classes that Jennifer really likes. Mrs. Waverly's is one of them. Jennifer loves music."

Before Lexi could think about all she had heard, Mrs. Drummond, the class advisor, called for their attention and it was nearly a half-hour and a mind-boggling amount of information later that Lexi and her friends were released to find their classes. Jennifer still had not come.

"We've got bookkeeping together, Lexi," Binky announced after studying her schedule. "And English." Then her face fell. "That's all though. I'd hoped we'd have lots of classes together."

"It's all right. We'll have plenty of time together after school," Lexi promised. "Right, Peggy?"

"I hope so, because the only class you and I share is history." She glanced at her watch. "And we'd better get going. Mr. Raddis is very fussy about being on time."

Binky waved goodbye and Peggy led Lexi toward the history room. When they reached the door Peggy expelled a little puff of air and a soft "Oh."

When Lexi peeked over her shoulder, she could see Jennifer sitting at the very back of the room. "You're going to be in on it," Peggy warned.

"In on what?"

"History. The third world war. Stubborn object—meaning Jennifer—meets immovable force. That's Mr. Raddis. I predict trouble."

Refusing to be sucked into Peggy's grim prediction, Lexi entered the room eagerly. Mr. Raddis was a cheerful-looking middle-aged man. Lexi liked him immediately.

"So you're new, Alexis Leighton," he murmured when she handed him a small white card from the office. "Welcome to Cedar River High."

"Thank you."

"You'd better find a seat. We have a lot to cover. More history is being made while we stand here talking."

Lexi had never thought of history quite like that before, and as Mr. Raddis began to talk, she marveled at how immediate and important he could make a hundred-year-old event seem. It wasn't until class was nearly over that Lexi happened to turn around and get a glimpse of Jennifer slouched low and miserable in the last row.

Her face was grim, her eyes staring straight ahead. Though she took no notes as Mr. Raddis spoke, she seemed to be listening intently—and hating every moment of it.

"See?" Lexi whispered to Peggy at the sound of the bell. "Jennifer didn't cause any trouble."

Lexi made her way to bookkeeping alone, glad for

a moment to consider what was going on around her. In class, Binky had saved her a seat. The hour went quickly and soon they were escaping into the corridor.

Noon hour came quickly. "Lexi! Binky! Wait up!" Jennifer's voice caught them just as they turned toward the lunchroom. "Can I join you?"

Much to Lexi's relief, Jennifer appeared relatively cheerful as she entered their conversation.

"Fish sticks? Already?"

"And green peas cooked until they're white."

"Did anyone grab any extra bread? There's some peanut butter on the other end of the table."

Lexi allowed the banter to flow around her, listening to snatches of conversation.

" . . . and if I make the Emerald Tones I have my parents' permission to go on tour. . . ."

" . . . but my biology instructor says we *have* to dissect something. If I have a choice, I'm going to pick a shark. If I have to even *touch* a frog I know I'll. . . ."

" . . . so Wanda told Marty what she'd heard from Ginny about what Debbie told her. . . ."

"Ready?" Jennifer stood up and peered into Lexi's face.

"I guess so. Are you? You haven't eaten anything."

Jennifer shrugged. "Not hungry, I guess."

"The chocolate pudding wasn't so bad."

Jennifer smiled weakly. "It's okay. My stomach is kind of queasy, that's all."

"Are you all right? Maybe you should go and see the nurse—"

"Nah. It's fine. I feel better already. I see Egg on

the other side of the room waving—I'll see you later."

Lexi picked up her tray and turned to Binky with a questioning expression marking her features. Binky shrugged helplessly. "It's just the way it is, Lexi. She never eats at school."

As Lexi crossed the crowded room, she marveled at how easily everyone seemed to accept Jennifer's obvious discomfort. But, Lexi reminded herself, she was new here. Maybe there were things she still didn't know about her friends.

She was so engrossed in her thoughts that Lexi didn't see the tall, dark-haired boy in front of her until she'd managed to tread on his heels and poke him in the back with her tray.

"I'm sorry! I didn't mean to . . . Jerry!" Her words came out in a gasp.

"Hi, Lexi. It's okay. I didn't need the backs of my shoes for anything anyway."

"Sorry."

He smiled. Jerry was thinner than the last time she'd seen him. It hadn't marred his athletic handsomeness. In fact, the newly angular bones of his face and the softer, more contemplative expression in his eyes made him more handsome.

"How are you?" she asked.

"Okay. Surviving. How's Ben?"

There was a tense, silent moment between them. Then Lexi smiled.

"Fine. Just fine. He never mentions the accident. It's like it never happened for Ben."

"Good." Jerry paused. "I wish it were that way for me."

Together they moved through the line to clear

their trays and emerged in the hallway on the other side.

"What's happening?" Lexi asked. She and her parents hadn't discussed what would become of Jerry. They'd only insisted that he be remembered in their prayers.

"I'm on juvenile probation," he admitted.

"What does that mean?"

"No extracurricular activities, for one thing." He looked regretful. "No football, no basketball, no school plays."

"I'm sorry."

"Hey! Don't be. I deserve it, Lexi. I almost killed your brother with that stupid stunt. I deserve all the punishment I get."

Lexi studied him from beneath her lowered lids. She didn't like this subdued, willing-to-be-punished Jerry any more than she'd liked the cocky, self-serving boy he'd been before the accident. Impulsively she asked, "Jerry, have your parents been home since the accident?" Lexi knew that they lived and worked far away and only came to Cedar River for brief visits.

His eyes flashed for a brief second. "No. Why should they? My aunt and uncle are 'handling' things. They can ground me just as well as my folks could."

"But wouldn't you like to talk to them?"

His shoulders went back in a swagger. "Talk? Nah. What's to talk about?"

Lexi didn't believe him for a minute. Couldn't *anyone* let their feelings show? First Jennifer, now Jerry.

"Nothing, I guess," she finally concluded. "You know best."

"Anyway, I'm busy. The judge said I had to do volunteer work in the community."

"Really? Like what?"

He gave a depreciating shrug. "I've been helping with the flower beds at the park. Now that fall is here, I suppose I'll get another job."

"Good luck," Lexi murmured.

"Yeah. You bet." A little bit of his familiar swagger returned. Sadly, Lexi watched him meander down the hall. Suddenly she felt very lonely for her old friends and her old school. Everything was too different here. There was so much she didn't understand.

Sighing and hoisting her books higher into her arms, Lexi set out to find her next class.

Chapter Three

"Where were you?" Jennifer's voice came accusingly across the hall. "Egg and I waited and you never showed up!" Jennifer was waiting impatiently near the English classroom.

"Sorry. I was talking to Jerry Randall."

"Oh, that explains it. How is Jerry?"

"I feel sorry for him. He doesn't seem very happy."

Jennifer stared at her friend. "That's just like you, Lexi—to feel sorry for the guy who almost killed your little brother."

"It was an accident, and Ben's all right." Lexi paused to consider her statement. "More all right than Jerry seems to be. . . ." But her words were lost on Jennifer, who had suddenly turned into the restroom just outside their classroom. Not knowing what else to do, Lexi followed her inside. "Jennifer? I think I'd better get to class before—What's wrong?"

Jennifer was emerging pale and shaky, her eyes suddenly red-rimmed. "Nothing. I just threw up."

Lexi's eyes grew wide. "I knew you should have gone to see the nurse! I'll go tell her that—"

"Don't bother." Jennifer's voice was oddly resigned and distant. "I always throw up before English class." She struggled to give a weak grin. "It's become as routine as doing homework."

"Could I get you something?"

"Skip it, Lexi. It's nothing. Really." Jennifer took a paper towel from the dispenser and ran it under cold water. She patted at her mouth and cheeks.

"But we need to know what it is!" Lexi persisted. "The school nurse could. . . ."

Jennifer stared at Lexi with an odd, appraising look. Finally she said, "Yeah, maybe you're right. A bug. That's it. So don't worry about it. I'll go right home after school and put my feet up. Okay?"

"Promise?"

Jennifer rolled her eyes and made a grimace. "I promise. If I don't, you can chop my hair off at the roots."

"You don't need to be so dramatic," Lexi chided. "I'm worried about you, that's all."

Jennifer looked at her for a long, silent moment. When she spoke, her voice was low and gruff. "I know. And I appreciate it—I really do. It's just that there's no way you can help." Then she turned and led the way out the door.

The English room was bright and sunny, with high, wide windows and two walls lined with books. There were posters on the bulletin boards—"Shakespeare was a bard, not a nerd" and "Let English Lit. Light Up Your Life." A sense of cheerful disarray permeated the room, and Lexi liked it immediately.

Mrs. Drummond stood at the desk greeting each

student individually. Only Jennifer seemed reluctant to respond to the friendly hello with a smile. Then the teacher turned her attention to Lexi.

"Hello. You must be new."

"Yes. I'm Alexis Leighton. I moved here from—"

"—Grover's Point. I know. I happen to have been a long-ago college roommate of your English teacher there. We had a long conversation about you."

"Oh?" Lexi said uneasily. She always *thought* Mrs. Lon had liked her, but you never knew. . . .

Mrs. Drummond smiled. "Mrs. Lon said you were one of her most promising students and that I would enjoy having you in my class."

Lexi's shoulders relaxed. "Oh, good, I just thought . . ."

Mrs. Drummond chuckled and her eyes squinted into an easy smile. "Of course, even if Mrs. Lon had told me you were a card-carrying lunatic, I would have been glad to meet you. Welcome to class."

A happy glow spread through Lexi. English had always been her favorite subject. With Mrs. Drummond as a teacher, no doubt that would continue.

Considering the friendly atmosphere of the classroom, Lexi couldn't figure out what Jennifer found to be so nervous about. She sat in the back of the classroom, her eyes cast downward, chewing on fingernails already raw and reddened at the edges.

The final bell had already rung when Mrs. Drummond announced, "Anyone who is interested in working on the school newspaper, please see me right now or stop back after school. I want to get a list of names so we can begin assigning positions and getting our reporters out on their beat. After all, the news doesn't wait for us to get organized! Here's a slip of paper on which you can . . ."

Lexi gladly took a slip. After putting her name on the line and gathering her books, Lexi glanced around the room, but Jennifer had already vanished. Neither did Lexi see her in the hallways later as she wove her way back to the English room, which was also the heart of the school newspaper.

Mrs. Drummond had called an informal meeting for those interested in being on staff to discuss the types of positions that were open. Already Lexi had several ideas she'd like to explore for the paper—if she was given the opportunity.

Egg was in the English room involved in a heated discussion with several boys Lexi didn't know. They were discussing the pluses and minuses of lifting weights over the summer to keep in shape. Lexi put her hand over her mouth to hide a smile. Scrawny Egg didn't look much like a weight lifter. His shape was more like one of the barbells.

Across the room in a huddle of girls sat Minda Hannaford holding court. Half a dozen rapt pairs of ears listened to every word she said about the *absolute necessity* of having both a fashion column and a gossip column in the school paper. Lexi deftly avoided both groups in favor of edging nearer the teacher's desk.

Mrs. Drummond was adept at handling controlled chaos, Lexi decided as the meeting progressed. She managed to break up Minda's group tactfully and co-mingle them with Egg and the athletes.

Lexi noticed that Egg found a seat beside Minda's. Was that the same Egg who had called Minda "stuck-up, conceited and self-important"? Lexi tucked that thought away for further consideration.

"As most of you know, we're going to expand the *River Review* this year. We've been given the go-ahead to produce four more pages."

Everyone clapped and hooted. A whistle rent the air at the back of the room.

"But, of course, that means more work."

Now the sounds were low moans and groans. "*And* more columns."

"Sports profiles!"

"Fashion!"

"Gossip!"

Mrs. Drummond looked around the room and her gaze settled on Lexi. "What? No input from our newest staffer? Maybe Lexi has some ideas from her last school that would help us improve the *Review*."

Lexi squirmed under the attention she was receiving. Still, she *had* glanced at the school paper, comparing it to her old school's paper. The *River Review* was much larger and they obviously had new and improved typesetting facilities. Still, Grover's Point's paper—*What's the Point?*—had seemed more interesting and lively.

She could feel an embarrassed burn racing up her neck to brighten her cheeks. "The biggest difference I've noticed between my old school paper and this one is the photos."

"Photos?" Mrs. Drummond echoed. "What do you mean?"

"Well, it's just that all the pictures in *Review* look so . . . posed."

"They're *supposed* to be posed, silly," Minda groused from the back of the room.

"I know that, but the Grover's Point paper also has lots of candid shots—kids just doing what they normally do around the school, funny shots of people when they don't expect it—humorous things. We had a photo column just like the columns you have for sports and news items. It was a collage of what had been happening in the school that week or month. It made the paper seem . . . cozy."

Lexi knew immediately that she'd chosen the wrong word. Minda gave a loud, unladylike snort. "*Cozy?* Who wants a 'cozy' school paper? How can we win prizes with cozy?"

Lexi bit her lip. When Minda quit talking, Lexi started to explain herself. "Maybe 'cozy' wasn't the right word, but whatever it was, it worked. Our paper won prizes all the time." Then Lexi had a sudden flash of brilliance. "For example, if you wanted to run a fashion column once in a while, who'd be interested if they couldn't *see* the fashions but only read about them? Wouldn't it be great to have a column about who's wearing what now? Candid shots would work in beautifully." Then, feeling as if she'd said too much, Lexi grew silent as the rest of the room burst into conversation.

"A fashion column illustrated with us! That's a great idea."

"Minda, you'd be in it every time, I just know it. Who else dresses like you do?"

"And we could do a photographic tour of the whole school over the year. I mean, really, who knows what the janitor does in the furnace room, anyway?"

"Yeah, and maybe we could get a shot of the guidance counselor when he puts his feet up on the desk and dozes off while he's administering aptitude tests."

"I thought four pages would be pretty hard to fill, but if we use more pictures . . ."

The idea grew like a prairie fire on a dry summer day. Soon everyone but Mrs. Drummond and Lexi were babbling excitedly about the possibilities.

Mrs. Drummond leaned over and murmured near her ear. "Good suggestion, Lexi; sounds as if we'll have to try it."

Lexi looked longingly at the group. She'd been *What's the Point?*'s chief photographer. Here, she doubted that she'd have any chance at all of being anything other than a go-fer or someone's assistant.

A noise at the door made everyone turn their heads.

"Sorry I'm late. Did I miss anything?"

Lexi's heart beat a little faster. She hadn't realized that Todd was on the paper staff.

"Ms. Leighton has given us a good idea for the paper this year. What do you think about adding some photos and taking a more casual approach to some of the shots—just to show what's happening around the school?"

"Sounds great to me," Todd said as he slid into a chair near Lexi's. "I've always thought those stiff-backed, stern-faced pictures everyone insisted I take were pretty dull."

Mrs. Drummond turned to Lexi. "You're idea has been okayed by our chief photographer, Lexi."

"Todd?" She swiveled to face him.

He gave her a wide grin. "Sure. I'm a man of many talents. I keep telling you that. Don't you believe me?"

"Too bad you don't like writing the copy that goes with your pictures, Todd," Mrs. Drummond chided gently. Then she turned to Lexi. "Perhaps you'd like to work on photos and captions with Todd—just to ease you into our newspaper style."

Lexi willed every fiber in her body not to jump up with a gleeful shout. It wouldn't do to make an idiot of herself even if she *was* absolutely delighted to be working with photography—and Todd. "Sounds great," she managed, hoping no one else noticed how her voice trembled.

"Good. Then that's taken care of. Mr. McNaughton, since you've had the most experience, you'll be in charge of layout as we discussed last spring."

Egg's head bobbed happily.

"Now, then, since we have two big items out of the way, what about these new columns you were so eagerly discussing . . ." Lexi scanned the room as the discussion progressed. So many strange, new faces, so many people to meet. She found herself sighing. Moving into a new town was overwhelming business—especially knowing that not everyone was happy to have her here.

Her gaze slid to Minda. The blond, blue-eyed girl was looking satisfied as a cat who'd consumed a saucer of cream. Mrs. Drummond had okayed a trial fashion column written by, of course, Minda herself and to be alternated with the breezy chitchat, or "gossip," column she'd started the year before.

Well, Lexi thought to herself, it was certainly safer to have Minda writing about inanimate things like fashion than newsy bits of gossip. She imagined that Minda could be deadly with a pen.

Meanwhile Egg had been edging his chair closer and closer to Minda's, making any excuse to lean forward and talk to her. Unfailingly, Minda ignored him.

When Mrs. Drummond asked for volunteers to hand out sample copies of some other school papers, Egg nearly fell out of his chair in his eagerness to volunteer. When he came to Minda's seat, he managed to brush his arm along the top of her shoulder as he handed her the paper. His reward was an irritated look, a sharp elbow jab in the stomach, and Minda's irate, "You don't have to be so clumsy, Egg. Watch what you're doing!"

Egg McNaughton and Minda Hannaford. An unlikely combination, Lexi mused. Obviously Minda thought so too.

"That's it for now, everyone," Mrs. Drummond concluded. "I think you all have enough to think about. Exact assignments will be posted tomorrow, but you all have a general idea of what's expected of you. Remember, our first task is the Homecoming issue. It's given to all the alumni who return, so you'll have a very particular audience. We want to look our best," Mrs. Drummond added as she closed her book.

With a loud scuffle, they all bolted from their chairs. Egg left the room close on Minda's heels, while Todd and Lexi followed at a more leisurely pace.

"So, I see you're a big hit," Todd observed.

"A hit?" Lexi retorted. "The only kind of 'hit' in that room was the one Minda wanted to give me."

He chuckled. "Don't pay any attention. Anyway," his blue eyes sparkled, "it looks as though Egg's getting more love-sick by the hour. Pretty soon Minda won't have time to think of anything but him."

"He's setting himself up for a heartbreak," Lexi observed. First Jennifer, now Egg. Everybody seemed set on a path toward destruction!

Chapter Four

"Have you heard who's going to run for Homecoming queen?"

"Not yet, but I did hear that the senior class already has their float idea."

"Not like last year's, I hope—that big black skunk with a tail made of wire mesh and the theme, 'Stink 'em out.'"

"I heard it's going to be worse this year."

"How could it be? A big bat and the slogan 'Flap on to victory'?"

"... or 'Bat a thousand, win the game.'"

"How about 'We're rabid for a victory'? Get it? Bats have rabies—rabid—you know . . ."

"This is the *dumbest* conversation I've ever heard!"

"No, I heard one dumber in math class today. You'll never believe what Frankie Hays asked . . ."

Todd groaned near Lexi's ear. "These people are all nuts. Why'd we ever think great minds like ours could work on the newspaper staff?"

Lexi grinned. "Actually, I like it."

Todd produced a slow and lazy smile. "You know, I do too."

"Do you have any good ideas for our first issue?" Lexi asked eagerly. She could feel her fingers twitching, wishing she already had her index finger on a shutter button and her eye at a viewfinder.

"Well," Todd began thoughtfully, "if you like the idea of a collage, maybe we should plan to do a 'Then and Now' sequence. I know there are lots of old photos in the files for the 'then' side. Once we pick out the pictures we want, we could duplicate them in a 'now' setting."

"If we find an old picture of someone wearing bobby socks and a poodle skirt stuffing books in her locker, we should get a current photo . . ."

" . . . of someone in a denim mini and an oversized jacket doing the same thing."

"The alumni could have fun looking for themselves and their classmates in the paper . . ."

" . . . and so would the current students." He threaded his fingers through his hair. "Sounds like a winner to me."

"Tell me about Homecoming, Todd. What's it like here?"

"You'll know all about it, Lexi, don't worry. We always do a series of Homecoming photos for the paper and the bulletin board at the entry to the school. You'll be taking pictures of everything that happens."

"Tell me more."

Todd shrugged. "Same old thing. A football game. A parade. A pep rally and coronation where we choose a Homecoming king and queen. And of course there's 'theme week.' "

"What's theme week?"

"Every day has a different theme—'Backward Day,' 'Hawaiian Day,' 'Blue and Gold Day,' 'Dress-Up Day.'" Seeing Lexi's perplexed expression, he added, "It's just like it sounds. You wear whatever is appropriate for the day—a Hawaiian shirt and shorts or a suit and tie."

"Or all your clothes backward?"

"Right."

"What does Minda think of that?" Lexi wondered. "Does it suit her sense of 'fashion'? "

Todd chuckled. "Nope, it doesn't. But everyone else in school does it, so if she refused to join in, she'd be the one out of style for the day."

"What about Jennifer?" Lexi murmured. "Does she take part?"

Todd looked at her in surprise. "Of course. Jennifer usually manages to find the wildest costumes of all. Why?"

"Oh, no reason," Lexi said evasively. "No reason at all."

Jennifer's personality was like that of a roller-coaster—up one minute and down the next. But *why*?

School had been in session only one week when the trouble started in English class.

"Are you done with your report?" Binky inquired nervously. "I'm so scared. I'm not sure I did this right. I really couldn't understand the directions."

"It was confusing," Lexi agreed. "I've never had to think about Shakespeare in modern-day terms before. It took me a long time to figure out what 'salad days' meant. I finally had to ask my dad. He said it means you're young. You know, green and tender."

"Oh, sick," Binky groaned. "No wonder I didn't understand what I was doing."

The girls entered the door of the English classroom and Lexi glanced around. There was a low hum in the room, a nervous buzz, like bees hovering over flowers. She could feel the tension in the air. Obviously, everyone was as nervous about the assignment as she was.

Everyone, that is, except Jennifer. She didn't seem concerned at all. She was sitting in the back of the room, gazing out the window, her feet propped on the chair of the desk next to her, her arms folded across her chest and her head tilted back and up as though she were looking at clouds.

"Look at her," Binky whispered; "do you think she's got this done?"

"Who knows?" Lexi shrugged. She couldn't figure anything out about Jennifer lately. Some days she was just like the girl she had met last summer— happy and carefree and full of fun. At other times she was so grumpy that Lexi couldn't think of a thing to say to her. Whatever was going on with Jennifer, Lexi was at a loss to understand.

When it came time to hand in the papers, Lexi drew her name quickly across the top of the page and handed it toward the front. Out of the corner of her eye, she noticed that Jennifer pulled a single sheet of paper out of a folder and passed it forward.

Mrs. Drummond leafed through the papers as they came forward, row by row, eyeing them casually, with an occasional nod of pleasure or a frown. When she came to the last row, Jennifer's row, she did the same, giving each assignment a cursory examination.

Suddenly she paused, the frown on her forehead deepening to a scowl as she pulled a single paper out of the pile and laid it on top of the rest. There was a long silence. When she spoke, her words were deadly quiet.

"Miss Golden? What's your idea here?"

Jennifer looked up casually. "Excuse me?" she said in a challenging voice. "I don't understand."

"I asked you to do a report on what terms we might use today and how Shakespeare might have said the same things. I don't see any of that on this page, Miss Golden."

"Oh, is *that* what you meant?" Jennifer managed a baffled expression, as if she hadn't understood the assignment at all. "Sorry about that."

The teacher's face darkened. "I was very explicit in my instructions, Miss Golden."

"Maybe, maybe not. I didn't understand them."

There was a corporate gasp throughout the room. What had gotten into Jennifer now?

"I'll see you after class at my desk," the teacher said coldly.

Instead of remaining silent, Jennifer squared her shoulders and said, "I have another class after this one. I can't stop at your desk."

"At my desk after class."

Jennifer looked directly at Mrs. Drummond. "No."

"It's either here or in the Principal's office, Miss Golden. Your choice."

At that, Jennifer seemed to realize that she had gone too far. "All right, I suppose," she growled moodily. "If I have to, but I don't want to be late for my next class."

For the rest of the hour, Lexi could barely pay attention to what was being said. When the bell rang she had only two sentences of notes in her notebook.

Each time Lexi had glanced back at Jennifer, she was in the same position—shoulders hunched, head bowed, fingers laced together over her notebook and pen on the top of her desk. There was an intense expression across her forehead, and she looked as if she was listening earnestly, as if her life depended upon it.

In the hallway after class, Binky came barreling up so that she nearly knocked Lexi into a row of lockers. "Did you hear what Jennifer said?"

"How could I miss it?" Lexi groaned.

"This happens every year. Seems like Jennifer comes to school just looking for trouble. She's been pretty good in History, I hear. And Home Ec.'s been fine, but Math . . ." Binky shook her head. "She's been awful in Math, refusing to do her assignments, saying they're dumb."

"Dumb?" Lexi echoed. Jennifer dared to tell her teacher that her assignments were dumb? The puzzle wore at Lexi until the dismissal bell rang and continued to disturb her as she walked home.

When she reached her house, she was relieved to find a note from her mother on the kitchen table saying that she and Ben had gone for groceries.

Enjoying the peaceful silence that pervaded the house, Lexi went to her room and opened her Bible once again to the book of Mark. Her fingers flew to the eleventh chapter, and she read one more time the words that she and Binky had discussed.

> If you only have faith in God—this is the absolute truth—you can say to this Mount of Olives, "Rise up and fall in the Mediterranean" and your command will be obeyed. All that's required is that you really believe and have no doubt. Listen to me! You can pray for *anything*, and *if you believe, you have it*; it's yours.

Lexi sank thoughtfully into the deep recesses of her chair. This was God's word telling her that she could ask for anything, anything at all, and have faith in knowing that God would provide her with an answer.

Folding her hands across her middle, Lexi bowed her head. "God, it's me, Lexi. I'm not praying about myself this time, Lord. Ben's doing great, and I'm fine. Thank you for that. Lord, this time, it's my friend Jennifer, who's in trouble. I don't know what's wrong with her, Lord. All I know, is that she's terribly unhappy and she's doing things to hurt herself."

As Lexi prayed, a feeling of peace came over her. Jennifer was in God's hands now, in the place where she was safest, and the only place Lexi could leave her.

She prayed quietly until the shadows of the evening overtook the house and she heard the sound of her mother's car in the driveway and Ben's cheerful voice singing slightly off-key. With a heart lighter and more unburdened than it had been all week, Lexi stood up and went to greet her family.

Cedar River High's Homecoming was the single most talked about topic in the entire school. Every class was busy preparing banners, choosing candidates, voting on ideas for parade entries and generally attempting to avoid the day-to-day work that the teachers were trying to press upon them.

Things were happening on a more personal level, too. Egg McNaughton had decided he wanted to take Minda Hannaford to the Cedar River Homecoming football game. He could've just as well decided to spend Christmas vacation visiting relatives on Mars.

Egg, however, was an eternal optimist where Minda was concerned. Every day, he approached her with a friendly smile and some new bit of friendly conversation, and every day she rebuffed him.

"He's a glutton for punishment," Lexi observed to Todd as they watched Egg make another attempt to capture Minda's attention. "Why won't he just give up and realize that she doesn't want to go out with him?"

"Go out with him?" Todd chuckled. "Minda doesn't even realize he wants to ask her out because she never speaks to him."

"He told me he'd been close to asking her twice," Lexi confided, "but then something or someone had gotten in the way."

Todd snorted unkindly. "Something or someone got in the way? I can guarantee that it's a someone."

"Oh?" Lexi murmured curiously.

"You mean you haven't heard?"

"Heard what?" Lexi asked blankly. Keeping up with the news in Cedar River was a full-time job.

"About Minda's latest love interest." Todd looked amused. "Or don't you keep up on things like that?"

"Not usually," Lexi admitted with a smile. "Of course, if *anything* happens to Minda, I seem to hear about it sooner or later. Who is it? Anyone I know?"

"Does the name Matt Windsor sound familiar?"

"Windsor? Matt? No, I don't think . . ." Then a light flashed into Lexi's brain. "You don't mean *the* Matt Windsor?"

"The one and only."

"But why?"

Todd shrugged. "Who knows? Maybe she's trying to make a statement about something."

"Of course, maybe he's very nice," Lexi ventured, "even if he does shave his head."

"Not all of it. Just the sides. He has hair on the top."

"Little spiked points of it," Lexi pointed out grimly. "And of course that little braided ducktail down the back."

Todd grinned even wider, seeming very amused by Minda's latest romantic choice. "Goes nicely with the earring, don't you think?"

"It's not funny, Todd," Lexi chided. "I think Matt Windsor is . . . scary."

Todd turned serious. "I've known Matt a long time, Lexi. He's a good guy—or he could be. This crazy stuff he's been doing to himself is fairly new. Three years ago he looked and acted just like me, an ordinary guy. Whatever's gotten into him lately is new."

Lexi's expression turned impish. "I'd hardly call you ordinary, Todd."

Todd ran his long fingers through his hair until it stood up on end in spiked clumps. "What do you think? How'd I look if I shaved a little off the sides?"

"Like you got your head caught in an electric pencil sharpener."

"Oh." He tamped his hair down with his hands. "Then you'd better tell Egg that."

"What has Egg got to do with this?"

Todd balanced a pencil on the tip of his index finger and idly watched it teeter back and forth. When it toppled to the floor he looked up. "Because after lunch today, Egg was in the men's room squashing his hair to his head and squinting into the mirror. I think he'd actually do it if it meant Minda would go out with him!"

Chapter Five

The whole world was going crazy.

Lexi leaned heavily against her elbows, her chin resting in cupped hands, staring out the window over her desk. A squirrel clung face down against a tree, flicking his tail and keeping a wary eye on the small boy stealthily crossing the yard toward him.

Ben's expression was as intent as the squirrel's as they eyed each other across the green expanse of grass. The closer Ben got, the more often the squirrel's tail flickered. Then, just when Ben was within pouncing distance, the little red animal turned tail and scampered up the tree just out of reach.

Lexi gave a weary smile. Ben and that squirrel had been playing games with each other all summer. Ben persistently stalked the squirrel, and the squirrel stayed just as persistently out of Ben's reach. No matter how many bread crumbs Ben laid out as part of his plan to trap the squirrel, it was still on the loose.

Lexi was beginning to feel as if she were part of a game being played out the same way. She was just as frustrated as Ben, desiring to pounce upon whatever illusive problem it was that caused Jennifer to act so strangely. She was sure that she could help—just by listening or offering some support—but Jennifer refused to be cornered any more easily than Ben's squirrel.

Lexi ran frustrated fingers through her hair. What was she supposed to *do* for someone who persistently refused help—or even refused to admit there was a problem? Her gaze skimmed the bookshelf near her desk and she pulled out a small, worn pamphlet on prayer. "Christians!" it began. "To pray is not only our right, but our duty."

Duty. Lexi tumbled the word around in her mind. Perhaps that's why she felt so burdened. Perhaps this was God's way of reminding her to pray for Jennifer.

"Lexi?"

"Come in, Mom." Lexi shifted in her chair to face the door.

"Are you all right?" Mrs. Leighton placed a stack of freshly folded clothing on Lexi's bed.

"Me? I'm fine."

"Someone else then?"

How did her mother *do* that? Lexi wondered. How did she always seem to know when something was going on in Lexi's life without asking a million intruding questions?

"It's Jennifer."

"She's still behaving strangely?"

"Yes. I can't figure it out. So far, all I've managed to discover is that there's a weird sort of pattern to her behavior."

"Oh?" Mrs. Leighton dropped lightly onto the bed

and curled her arms around her knees, a pose Lexi often adopted.

"She has the most trouble in English class," Lexi began. "And Peggy tells me that she's the most cheerful in Home Ec. She's very quiet in history and listens very intently—like she's mentally recording everything that's said."

"We've all had favorite classes, Lexi, perhaps she just—"

"I know I have favorites, but I don't cause trouble in all the rest!"

"True," Mrs. Leighton acquiesced. "Maybe for now praying for Jennifer is the only thing you can do."

"I have, Mom. I really have."

"Just remember, Lexi, when you're praying, don't limit God. Turn it all over to Him. After all, He's the One who can do miracles."

"Okay. Thanks."

Her mother nodded. "You're welcome." She paused in the doorway. "Lexi, maybe it wouldn't hurt to go over to Jennifer's and have a talk with her. Surely she knows how worried you are about her. Perhaps she's ready to tell you what's wrong."

Lexi gave her mother a doubtful stare. "I don't think so, Mom. Sometimes it's like talking to a stranger."

"When we're at our lowest and most uncooperative, sometimes that's when we need our friends the most."

Lexi nodded slowly. It made sense. The unlovable need love the most. She picked a sweat shirt from the pile of clean laundry on her bed and pulled it roughly over her head.

"Here I come, Jennifer," she muttered to herself, "whether you're ready or not!"

Mrs. Golden, at least, seemed pleased to see Lexi.

"Jennifer is upstairs in her room, Lexi. I'm sure she'll be delighted to see you."

I'm not so sure about that.

"She spends far too much time in her room these days." A worried crease marred Mrs. Golden's forehead. "She's much more outgoing and lighthearted in the summer." Then the worried expression fled. "But, of course, I suppose most students are that way. School can be so difficult, you know."

Yes, but not THAT difficult, Lexi thought. Aloud, she said, "We all have good and bad days, I guess."

"Well, my dear, I'm just glad you and Jennifer are friends." Mrs. Golden patted Lexi's cheek fondly. "She really does consider you her best friend."

Why then, Lexi wondered as she climbed the steps to the second floor, *doesn't she confide in me?*

Lexi paused a moment at the door before knocking. Music was playing softly on the other side. She drew a breath and knocked on the door.

"Come in."

Jennifer was lying on her back, legs and arms spread out, staring at the ceiling.

"Hi."

Jennifer turned her head sharply to look at the doorway. "Oh. It's you."

"I came to visit."

"Oh."

Lexi chewed at her lower lip. This wasn't off to a very good start.

"What are you doing?"

"Staring at the ceiling."

"I see that. Why?"

Swiftly, Jennifer sat up and slid off the bed. When she stood up, she held a bundle of posters in her hand. "These. I'm thinking of papering my ceiling. What do you think?"

Lexi blinked in surprise. "You mean you weren't lying there moping?"

"No. Why should I?" Jennifer busied herself spreading the posters across the bed. "I was just downtown and found this great sale. Look at these— three for a dollar! I almost bought them at full price last month!" She surveyed her purchases with obvious glee. "I can't believe I was this lucky!"

Jennifer gave a happy twirl around the room. "Now that you're here, you can help me put them up. Thumbtacks would be best, I think. Masking tape will never hold these and if one of them falls down in the middle of the night, I'll be scared out of my wits. You hold this and I'll go get a stepladder."

Lexi was left standing in the middle of the room clutching a handful of posters and staring perplexedly at the door through which Jennifer had disappeared.

Baffled by the one hundred eighty degree twist in Jennifer's personality, Lexi dropped onto the bed and stared around the room.

She could have been sitting in the stereo department of one of the stores in the Cedar River Mall, Lexi decided. Jennifer had a sound system that rivaled Minda Hannaford's—and that was no small feat, considering the amount of money Minda was allowed to spend.

While the walls of Lexi's room were filled with overstuffed bookshelves, Jennifer's housed a sleek wall unit with a turntable, tape deck, compact disc player, speakers, amplifiers and a few gadgets Lexi didn't even recognize. Records, tapes and discs filled the shelves in an orderly hodge-podge. A small color television sat on Jennifer's bedside table and an elaborate synthesizer rested across the lid of a wicker chest. Gadgets were everywhere—but not a single book or magazine to be seen.

Jennifer burst into the room waving a cardboard paper of thumbtacks. Her blond hair swung in a silky sheet across her shoulders, moving as she gestured. "This should do it. I've got the ladder in the hall. If you'll hold it steady, I can put up the posters."

Lexi found herself recruited into Jennifer's decorating plans as easily and naturally as in the days before school and Jennifer's odd behavior had started.

When the last of the posters was in place and they were admiring the work over a plate of nachos, Lexi finally mustered the courage to ask what had been on her mind.

"Jennifer?"

"Yeah?" She flipped her bangs from her eyes and popped another nacho into her mouth.

"Could I ask you something?"

"Depends on what it is." Jennifer's expression grew wary.

"It's school. What's going on?"

"Nothing. Nothing at all." Jennifer picked at the food in front of her.

"You can't expect me to believe that, Jen. I can see for myself."

"So then you figure it out." Her expression grew sullen. "I don't want to talk about it."

"Then there *is* something wrong! Please," Lexi pleaded, "let me help you. English class has been a disaster. You and Mrs. Drummond have been at each other's throats since the first day. Why?"

"I just happen to not like English, and I don't keep it to myself, that's all." Jennifer's chin thrust forward defiantly.

"You mean you aren't going to tell me."

"I mean, *there's nothing wrong*. Don't get into it, Lexi."

Rather than press further and risk ruining the happy afternoon they'd had, Lexi changed the subject. "Have you seen much of Egg lately?"

Sensing that Lexi had given up on her quest for information, Jennifer gave a weak smile. "No, not really. Unless, of course, he's attached to Minda's heels."

"So you've noticed that too."

"I'd have to be blind not to. Poor Egg. He's going to have his heart broken into a million pieces." Jennifer scowled. "I don't know what he sees in her anyway. I wouldn't like someone who hated me."

"Minda's beautiful and rich—and can also be very nice when she wants to be. She's popular too. Apparently Egg can't resist."

"The only time she pays any attention to him is when she wants him to do something for her. Yesterday I saw him carrying chairs into the gymnasium."

"So?"

"So, it was Minda's job to put out extra chairs for the Student Council meeting."

"Oh."

"I don't like the way she's using him," Jennifer commented.

Lexi shrugged. "He'll just have to learn the hard way what Minda is like." She paused a moment to remember her own first encounter with Minda. "Just like the rest of us did."

"Well, Egg is going to crack when he finds out." Jennifer grinned. "Pardon the pun."

Lexi laughed and said, "There's time to do some shopping today, Jenna. What do you think? A couple of hours at the mall?"

"Need you say more?" Jennifer jumped to her feet. "Maybe we'll run into Binky and Peggy. They were going to look for a birthday present for Peggy's mother."

"Let's go." Lexi glanced at her watch. "There's a bus in ten minutes."

Maybe, just maybe, Lexi thought to herself as they raced for the front door, *this meant that the old Jennifer was back.*

Chapter Six

The Cedarwood Mall parking lot was congested with cars and traffic. "Where do all these people come from?" Jennifer wondered aloud.

"Same place you and I do, I suppose," Lexi murmured. "They're all looking for something to do on a Saturday afternoon."

Jennifer stood in the arch that spanned the entryway to the mall and looked up, her hands on her hips, her eyes wide. "I wonder what people did for entertainment before there were malls?"

Lexi chuckled. "I don't know. They probably read books."

Jennifer's nose wrinkled in an expression of distaste. "Well, I'm certainly glad that I wasn't around then."

They hadn't been strolling up and down the aisles for more than ten minutes when they heard Peggy's and Binky's familiar voices calling from behind them. "Lexi! Jennifer! Wait up."

"What are you doing here?" Binky bubbled. "I didn't think you were coming out today."

"Lexi helped me hang posters on the ceiling of my bedroom," Jennifer explained. "Then we decided to shop for a little while."

"Good!" Peggy exclaimed. "I'm glad we saw you. We found a present for my mom"—she patted her pocket, where a tiny bulge the size of a small jewelry box was tucked—"and now we were just going down to Bridger's for a shake. Want to join us?"

"Sure, why not?" Lexi dug in the pocket of her jeans. "I think I have enough money."

"My treat," Jennifer announced. "This has been a great day. I can spend all the money I saved from those posters I got on sale." No one questioned Jennifer's financial logic as they made their way to the malt shop at the far corner of the mall.

When they emerged some moments later, Lexi nearly tripped on a small boy darting from behind a planter into her path. "Whoa," she muttered, "it's getting crowded in here."

"Yeah, let's make a break for it," Jennifer agreed. "I think I'm getting claustrophobic."

"Fine with me," Peggy echoed. "Where do you want to go?"

"I hear there's a new display at the museum. Does anybody want to go and take a look at it?"

"The museum?" Binky groaned. "Who goes to a museum on a Saturday afternoon?"

"I do, for one," Lexi laughed. "I love it there. Besides, I want to see the new dinosaur displays."

"Dinosaurs? Really?" Binky said. "Well, that might be kinda fun."

"Okay, come on then. What are we waiting for?" Lexi led the way to the bus.

At the museum, the lines were considerably shorter than at the mall. Jennifer had been very silent, but Lexi had hardly noticed because of Peggy and Binky's chatter. "Maybe I'll just go home," Jennifer finally said softly. "I'm not sure I really want to—"

"Of course you want to come in. It's great. Dinosaurs. You'll love it!" Lexi enthused. "Don't tell me you've never been here before."

Jennifer shrugged. "A couple times. It was all right, I guess."

"Well, come on. I think you'll be surprised."

The four girls flashed their student cards and trooped into the dim, cool recesses of the Cedar River Museum. The two-story hallways that usually stood empty were filled today with the massive skeleton of a prehistoric creature.

"Wow," Binky muttered. "Huge!"

"Told you you'd like it," Lexi chuckled. "Come on, there's a big sign over here telling us who this guy was and when he lived."

Peggy and Binky followed Lexi while Jennifer drifted off on her own to view the model of a pterodactyl, which had been set up on the side wall. It was several minutes before Lexi realized that Jennifer was no longer with them.

"Where'd she go?" Peggy muttered. "She was over there the last time I looked."

"She must have gone on into the other part of the museum," Lexi observed. "Let's go find her."

When they reached Jennifer, she was staring in fascination at a display of antique radios. "Look at these things," she murmured as the three girls approached her. "Look at how big they are!" She pulled her tiny Sony walkman out of her pocket and held it up for comparison. "They've come a long way with radios, haven't they?"

"You mean you're more interested in radios than dinosaurs?" Binky wondered.

"Sure," Jennifer enthused. "Just think of all the things you can learn from a radio. You get the news and the weather, the latest music and if you listen to the late evening shows, you can hear books and—"

"So what?" Binky said. "Who wants to hear books on the radio? I mean, really, if you're so crazy about books, just go to the library and check them out."

Jennifer's expression darkened. "Yeah, why not?" she finally muttered. "I'm just dumb to like radios. I know. I get it. I know what you're trying to say."

Binky blinked rapidly, her eyes wide and regretful. "That's not what I meant at all, Jennifer. I just meant that—"

"I know what you meant. I can hear it. You think it's stupid that I like to look at radios more than I like to look at dinosaurs. Well, I'm not stupid, no matter what you think. No matter what *anyone* thinks."

"But, Jennifer, I—" Binky stretched a thin hand toward the angry girl, but already, Jennifer was walking away from the startled threesome. When she turned back, her blue eyes were filled.

"I've gotta go. There's something I want to listen to on the *radio*. I'm sure you guys can do the rest of this museum without me."

"I didn't mean for that to happen!" Binky wailed as Jennifer disappeared around a corner.

"Forget it," Peggy consoled. "Jennifer's just been so . . . weird lately."

Jennifer was still on Lexi's mind Monday afternoon when she met Todd in the hallway in front of the gymnasium.

"Hi," he greeted her, flashing a wide pleased-to-see-you grin. "Are you ready for tryouts?"

"I don't know. I'm not sure I should have let you talk me into it."

Todd had managed to convince Lexi to try out for the Homecoming skits that were to be presented the night of the coronation. "I'm really not that fond of making a fool of myself."

Todd laughed out loud. "Who is? It's all just for fun, though. Besides, I helped write some of the skits this year. I know which parts we need to try out for."

"Ho-hooo," Lexi murmured. "There's method to your madness."

"You bet. Just stick with me and we'll have a great time."

That statement was hard for Lexi to deny. When she was with Todd, she always had a wonderful time. Tryouts for the skits were no different. At his advice, she tried out as a member of the royal court while he tried out for the part of Coach Derrick, strutting and bellering across the stage in a very coach-like fashion. Everyone on the skit committee was laughing so hard, tears were rolling down their cheeks by the time Todd finished his imitation of their beloved, but eccentric, coach. In the hallway after Todd's performance, Todd and Lexi ran into Jennifer, stuffing school books into her locker.

"Hi, kiddo. Are you gonna go to tryouts?" Todd

greeted her cheerfully, ignoring the sour look on Jennifer's face.

"Tryouts?" Jennifer echoed blankly.

"For the Homecoming skit. It's gonna be great. I helped write it." Todd's smile was wide and irresistible.

She gave a bleak flicker of a smile. "No, I don't think so. Not this year."

"Really?" Todd asked, surprised. "But you loved the summer musical we did so much. I thought for sure that—"

"I said no, Todd. Not this year."

"All right. It's up to you," Todd muttered.

Without another word, Jennifer turned and walked toward the exit. When her rigid back disappeared through the doorway, Todd turned to Lexi. "What's wrong with her?"

Lexi shrugged. "Got me. I've been wondering every day since school started what she's going to do next. Something's wrong, Todd, and I have no idea what it is."

His brow furrowed. "Well, you know, Jennifer's always been pretty sober during school. I always thought she loosened up during the summer. She's really a good kid."

"I know that." Before Lexi could sink into the doldrums she'd been feeling over Jennifer's behavior, Egg came rushing up beside them.

"Is it too late?" he gasped. "Is it too late to try out for the skits?"

"No, I don't think so," Todd said. "Why? I didn't think you were interested in this kind of thing, Egg."

Egg had the grace to blush. "I haven't been, until now."

"Oh? And what caused this big change?" Todd asked impishly.

"No special reason. Just thought it might be fun."

"Fun, huh?" From the corner of her eye, Lexi could see Minda entering the gymnasium by the far door. All the puzzle pieces were fitting into place.

"Well, please don't let us stop you," Todd said. "I'm sure there are people inside that you'd want to . . . ahem . . . talk to."

The tips of Egg's ears were a bright, transparent pink as he dodged through the double wooden doors that led to the gym. Todd's laughter followed him.

"Now, was that necessary?" Lexi chided gently. "Poor Egg is so embarrassed."

Todd snorted. "He should be. I don't know what he's got in his mind chasing Minda like that. Just like a dog chasing a car. The question always is, what is he going to do with it if he ever catches it?"

"Todd!" Lexi gasped, laughing.

"It's true. Egg's not very experienced where women are concerned. Even if Minda agreed to go with him, poor old Egg wouldn't know where to take her or how to entertain her. Minda's a little spoiled, you know."

Lexi winced. She knew better than anyone how spoiled Minda could act. Still, if Egg wanted to make a fool of himself in the Homecoming skit just to be near Minda, that was his choice.

On Tuesday afternoon Todd met Lexi at the front door with a camera draped around his neck and an eager expression on his face. "Hi, how's my right-hand photographer?"

"All right," Lexi laughed. "You look like you're about to go on a shooting expedition."

"Just getting ready for Homecoming week," Todd chuckled. "You never know when you might see something you want to catch on film."

"The only thing I need to catch on film right now are some facts about English," Lexi groaned. "Mrs. Drummond has really been piling on the homework."

Todd nodded in commiseration. "Yeah, I've heard that class is pretty tough going this year. Good luck."

Lexi nodded grimly. She was having trouble getting through all the reading assignments. The fact that she loved to read meant that there must be others who were really struggling with that particular class. Her thoughts went immediately to Jennifer, who spent most of the English hour with her head bowed and her hands folded over her notebook, appearing to listen or to sleep—Lexi wasn't quite sure which.

Class was the same today as it had been for several days. Volumes and volumes of complex notes on the large reading assignment. The only difference was that at the end of the hour, Mrs. Drummond looked up, closed her assignment book, and said, "I believe you students are ready to take your first test."

Groans of dismay filled the room.

"Already?"

"So soon into the semester?"

"We've hardly had time to . . ."

"I don't understand this Shakespeare dude."

"We need a little more time to discuss the . . ."

Lexi felt a swelling sense of foreboding. This was going to be a tough test. There was no doubt about that.

She turned her head and looked beneath half-lowered lids at Jennifer. While the others were complaining about the upcoming test, Jennifer remained silent and pale. Lexi felt nervous about the test, but Jennifer looked downright frightened.

"Please God, don't let her do anything stupid," Lexi petitioned, afraid that Jennifer might pull one of the nonsensical stunts she had performed earlier in the week when she had protested an assignment. Today, however, she was very quiet, and when the class bell rang, she had vanished into the hallway before Lexi could reach her. Thoughtfully, Lexi exchanged the books in her locker.

The test was to be the Tuesday prior to Homecoming weekend. Lexi winced. *That means one week from today.* It was a rotten trick to play, scheduling such a huge and important test just before Homecoming. Still, there would be plenty of time to study if she started tonight, but that meant her picture-taking would be on the back burner for next week.

Chapter Seven

It hardly seemed appropriate to take such an important test dressed in the outlandish clothes that the students were wearing.

For "backward" day, Lexi created a hat that rode on the back of her skull and looked like a face riding backward on her head. Then, when she turned all her clothes around and wore them backward, it looked as if there were a face walking down the hall backward, no matter which direction she was going.

The atmosphere in the hallway near the English room was grim.

"Are you ready for this?" Binky asked Lexi. A note of nervousness made her voice quaver.

"I'm not sure you can ever be ready for this," Lexi replied. "I stayed up half the night, and the longer I studied, the more fuzzy everything became."

"I know exactly what you mean," Binky moaned. "The same thing happened to me. About two A.M., I got Hamlet and Othello all turned around and by three, I couldn't even remember who Lady Macbeth was. Why do we have to start out by studying Shakespeare? We should have left him for last." She groaned again. "Whatever happened to classes without homework?"

Lexi shrugged. "I think they ended about third grade."

Binky plucked at the sleeve of her backward blouse. "You're probably right. I knew Peter Pan had a good idea—it was smart to never grow up."

"I wonder if Jennifer studied," Lexi murmured softly. "Have you seen her today?"

Binky shook her head. "Nope, not anywhere. Usually we arrive about the same time, but her locker hadn't been opened when I was there last. There was still some crepe paper strung through the lock."

The entire school looked like one big Homecoming party with the streamers and ribbons and helium-filled balloons practically everywhere. Someone had patiently tied crepe paper ribbons on the handle of each locker, and Lexi had taken a picture of them for the yearbook.

Then Binky's elbow in her side signaled Lexi that something was going on. "Here she comes."

Lexi glanced up to see Jennifer moving slowly down the hall. She'd made only a small concession to the Homecoming festivities, wearing blue jeans and a gold sweat shirt turned backwards. Her blond hair was pulled back into a tight french braid woven with blue and gold ribbons.

"Hi! Are you ready?" Binky asked cheerfully.

"Ready for what?"

"The English test, of course."

"Oh, that."

Roughly, she pulled the ribbon away from her locker door, spun out the combination and removed her books. "I'll never be ready for that." Then, as if she had said everything that either of them needed to know, she stocked off down the hall. Her shoulders were hunched forward and her knees slightly bent, as if she were walking into a strong wind. Binky whistled low under her breath.

"She's in a baaaad mood today."

Lexi felt Todd nudging her elbow. "Come on, I'll walk you to class."

Finally she was able to push all thoughts of Jennifer to the back of her mind. Today she had all of Hamlet and Othello and Romeo and Juliet's problems on her mind. Jennifer's would simply have to wait.

The test was even more difficult than Lexi had anticipated. Forty-five minutes into the hour, Lexi glanced worriedly at the clock. A trickle of nervous perspiration meandered down her spine and she wiped the back of her hand across her forehead as she glanced around the room. Everyone seemed to be as intent on his paper as she. Everyone, that is, except for Jennifer.

Her features were relaxed and her pencil seemed to be flying easily across the page in long strokes. Lexi shook her head and arched her eyebrows in surprise. All the studying she'd done had still left her with some gaps of information. She wondered how Jennifer could have managed to take it all in, particularly since she refused to take notes of any kind in class.

"There are ten minutes left in the hour," the teacher said. "Please keep this in mind when you're finishing up your test."

Lexi and every other student groaned at the announcement.

Only ten minutes, and she still had two essay questions left. How could she finish in that amount of time?

Just as a sense of panic began to overtake Lexi, Jennifer stood up. She walked nonchalantly to the front of the room, laid her test paper face down on the teacher's desk and returned to her place.

Lexi glanced quickly at her own paper. She was working as quickly as she could and still was running out of time. With renewed energy, Lexi's pencil flew across the page and she finished the final paragraph of the last essay question as the bell rang. With a rush of papers and shuffling footsteps, the room emptied.

Lexi found Jennifer by her locker in the hallway. "How'd you do that?" she wondered aloud.

"Do what?" Jennifer replied.

"Finish so early. I thought I was never going to get through that test."

"Oh, that."

"When I saw you hand your paper in, I nearly panicked," Lexi admitted. "I could have used another half hour."

"Not me," Jennifer retorted.

"What did you think about that question about—" Lexi began.

Before she could complete her question, Jennifer turned and said, "Listen, Lexi, I've gotta go, okay? I'm not really fond of rehashing test questions anyway. I figure, once they're done, they're done. I don't look back." With that, she slammed her locker shut, readjusted the armful of books she was carrying, and gave Lexi a small smile. "See you later, okay?"

There was nothing for Lexi to do but nod and murmur "okay" in response.

Some hours later, after the Leightons had finished their evening meal, Lexi sat down on the porch, propped up her feet, tipped her head back, and closed her eyes.

It was still very warm for a September evening and Lexi could hear the sound of a baseball game being played in the empty lot near the end of the street.

Ben sat quietly next to her, arranging brightly colored buttons from his button box in a pattern on the porch floor.

Lexi's father had been called away on an emergency concerning a German shepherd that had been hit by a Volkswagen.

It was a peaceful evening and Lexi refused to mar it by thinking of the dreadful test she'd taken that afternoon or the photographs she needed to have developed prior to her next newspaper deadline.

Then she heard her mother's footsteps moving from inside the house toward the front door.

"Lexi? Is this your sweater?"

Lexi looked up at the white cardigan in her mother's hands. "No. I think that belongs to Jennifer. She was wearing it the other evening when she stopped by."

"Why don't you run it over to her? Even if Jennifer hasn't missed it, no doubt her mother has. Besides, if I put it in our closet, we'll forget about it."

Slowly Lexi lifted her legs and dropped them to the porch floor. "I suppose. It's a nice night for a walk anyway."

"Thanks." Mrs. Leighton turned her attention to Lexi's little brother. "Come on, Ben. It's time for a bath and bed."

"Ben's busy," he protested. "Busy with buttons."

"You can do your buttons later, Ben. Come on, bath time."

Ben muttered a disgruntled complaint, but obediently gathered the buttons and dropped them into the small wooden box he kept them in. "Ben's coming," he finally announced.

Lexi smiled at her little brother. He'd been at the academy for the handicapped only a few days, but she could already see changes in him. He was more confident, more self-assured, and more independent.

She remembered the terrible struggle her mom had before she finally realized that enrolling Ben full time in the academy was the very best thing for him.

"Why is it," Lexi wondered aloud, "that so many right decisions are also the very hardest decisions to make?"

The Golden household was very quiet, but Lexi rang the doorbell and was soon rewarded with the sound of footsteps on the stairs. The front door flew open and Jennifer stood framed in the doorway. "Yeah, what do you want?"

Lexi's eyes widened. "Nice greeting. I'm glad you're happy to see me."

Jennifer's eyes flickered. "Sorry. I didn't mean it to sound like that."

"May I come in?" Lexi asked. "You left your sweater at my house."

"Oh, yeah," Jennifer pushed open the screen door. Silently, she took the cardigan from Lexi's hand and tossed it over the back of a chair.

"Something wrong?" Lexi ventured, knowing full well how Jennifer hated to be asked that question.

"Yes. No. I don't know," Jennifer said unhappily. "Who knows?"

"Anything I can help you with?" Lexi offered. "I'm a pretty good listener."

A tiny half smile twisted at the corner of Jennifer's lips. "I know you are, Lexi. Thanks, but no thanks. There's nothing you can do."

The two girls made their way to the top of the stairs and entered Jennifer's bedroom. Once again, Lexi was struck by the alarming number of gadgets and wild posters that Jennifer had hanging around the room. "I don't mean to nag," Lexi began, "but I meant it. If there's anything you'd like to tell me . . ."

Jennifer flopped onto her head, stomach first, folded her arms across one another and rested her chin on her wrist. "Frankly," Jennifer finally said, "I'm waiting for the trouble to start."

Lexi looked at her friend puzzled. "Trouble? What kind of trouble?"

"School trouble," Jennifer said. There was a resigned tone in her voice that alarmed Lexi. "With me, there's always school trouble."

"Are you talking about the English test today?" Lexi wondered. She could think of nothing else that would make Jennifer look so miserable. Still, Jennifer had been the first in the class to finish the test, so perhaps she hadn't found it as difficult as Lexi had.

"You've got it," Jennifer tried to be flippant, but failed miserably.

"But I was sure you'd aced it. You finished so early and—"

"Don't let appearances fool you, Lexi. The only reason I finished early was because I didn't write the test."

"But that's not possible. I saw you writing."

Jennifer snorted and rolled to her back. "You saw me doodling. I'm sure I turned in the most attractively decorated test paper in the entire class."

Lexi dropped to the bed next to Jennifer. "But why?"

A defiant, rebellious light sprang to Jennifer's eyes. "Because I didn't feel like taking that test, that's all."

"You didn't feel like it so you didn't write it?"

"That's what I said." Jennifer's chin jutted forward defiantly. "And they can't make me take it. No one can."

"But you're a student, Jennifer," Lexi began.

"Tell me about it. I hate it."

The silence between the two girls was so thick Lexi felt as if she could reach out and touch it. Then, in the farthest parts of the house, a telephone rang.

Neither girl spoke. After three rings, the telephone bell fell silent. Jennifer's eyes darted nervously from side to side.

"Somebody must've gotten it. Are your parents home?" Lexi wondered.

Jennifer nodded in the affirmative. "They're out on the deck with our next-door neighbors."

It was as though Lexi's mind had shut itself off and she were viewing an empty computer screen. She simply couldn't think of a thing to say. The two girls sat silently, staring at each other until the sound of footsteps on the stairway caused them both to turn and look through the open door of Jennifer's room. Jennifer's father came up the stairway first and her mother followed closely at his heels.

Lester Golden was a large man of Scandinavian descent. His shoulders were wide and well-muscled. His skin was tan from being outdoors and he wore his pale blond hair cropped short. He looked very much like his daughter.

Behind him came Jennifer's mother, also blond, but small boned and petite. Normally, Mrs. Golden's personality was warm and friendly, like rays of sunshine on a cloudy day. She, too, had blue eyes and telltale smile lines that creased at their corners, but tonight, neither Mr. nor Mrs. Golden was smiling.

"Jennifer, we need to talk to you," Mr. Golden began.

"Did the neighbors go home?"

"Yes. We asked them to leave." His eyes trailed to Lexi.

Awkwardly she stood up. "Well, Jennifer, maybe I should be going too. I've got lots of—"

"Don't leave. I want you to stay."

"But, your parents—"

"Never mind. I want you to stay."

"What we have to say is rather personal, Jennifer. I think it would be best if Lexi left." Mrs. Golden cast worried glances between her daughter and her friend.

Jennifer's eyes narrowed to an ugly squint.

"It's okay, Jennifer. Really. I have to be going," Lexi hurried to assure her friend.

Jennifer's hand shot out and grasped Lexi's arm.

"Maybe she should stay," Mrs. Golden said to her husband. "Maybe she could answer some, you know . . . questions." Lexi knew immediately that she was trapped.

"That was Mrs. Drummond on the phone, Jennifer. She was just grading the test that you took today."

"So?" Jennifer said defiantly. "What about it?"

"Don't you have something to say for yourself, Jennifer?"

If Lexi could have closed her eyes and wished herself out of this room and out of this house, she would have done so. As it was, she was trapped between two pairs of glaring, angry blue eyes.

"It's dumb. It's boring. I don't like Shakespeare. Who cares about something that was written four hundred years ago? Not me." Jennifer's belligerent eyes strayed to the wall.

"Enough!" Mr. Golden's voice was a low roar. "You should have thought how much you valued your stereo equipment before you chose not to write a test. There will be no more listening to music or playing with any of your electronic gadgets until this test is made up. While you're under this roof, you do not have the privilege of picking and choosing what you will or will not answer in class. Your television and your stereo equipment are off limits for the next thirty days."

"Thirty days!" Jennifer's voice was panic-stricken. "I can't be without—"

"Thirty days, Jennifer. That's my final word. Do you understand me?"

"Oh, I understand, all right. Just because I didn't write one lousy little test, you think you can take away everything that's important to me!"

"I think I'd better be going," Lexi murmured. Gently she placed her hand on top of Jennifer's and unwound the white-knuckled grip. "This is something you and your parents have to settle without me, Jen."

"Come, dear, I'll walk you to the door," Mrs. Golden offered nervously. "Perhaps Jennifer and her father need to be alone for a few moments."

On the stairway, Mrs. Golden turned to Lexi with tears in her eyes. "I'm sorry you had to be here to see that, Lexi. We've talked till we're blue in the face. Perhaps the only thing left to do is punish her. What else will jar her out of this horribly rebellious stage she's in?"

Lexi was no expert on human nature, but she doubted that harsh punishment was going to help Jennifer. Lexi could see Jennifer was hurting, but how could she help if she didn't know why?

Chapter Eight

"WE TAKE TRADE-INS" the sign on the furniture store boasted. "WHATEVER YOU HAVE TO TRADE—WE'RE INTERESTED."

"I wonder if that includes brothers," Binky grumbled as she and Lexi passed by the store windows packed full with davenports, wing-backed chairs and china cabinets. "I think my mom would be just as happy with a new dining room table as she is with Egg. I know I sure would be."

"Brother troubles?" Lexi chuckled. "Or are you that desperate for a new table?"

"He's turned weird, Lexi. Really, scary, far-out weird."

This time Lexi laughed out loud. "Egg's been weird since the first day I met him. That's part of his charm."

"You don't understand. He's . . ." Binky began to whistle an eerie tune, then said, "spooky, creepy, ready-for-the-institution weird."

"So tell me about it."

The girls were on their way home from an afternoon at the public library. The air was crisp and fall-like, the autumn sun heightening every color to its clearest, most pristine hue.

"You know Egg—the old Egg—happy, carefree, never really caring what other people thought."

Lexi nodded. Neither Egg nor Binky could be faulted for wearing clothing that was too expensive or for having too much pocket money. Still, they were outgoing, friendly people, unconcerned by how much money their father made—or didn't make. It was part of what she liked best about them.

"All of a sudden, that's all he thinks about." Binky's tone was morose. "He's been complaining to Dad about not making enough money and he tells Mom she should keep the house cleaner and . . ." Binky paused to sniffle, "He tells me that if I don't care how I look in school, then at least dress up for *his* sake."

"Egg said that?" Lexi gasped. "I can't believe it!"

"Believe it, all right," Binky muttered as she glanced longingly at the storefront windows. "I'd trade him in for a used vacuum cleaner right now. Or carpet remnants. Or . . ." She headed for the door.

Lexi grabbed her by the arm. "Or what? What have you got in that funny little head of yours, Binky?"

"I was just going to see if they had any packing boxes. Maybe we could ship Egg to Grandma's until he snaps out of this 'stage' Mom says he's in."

"That won't solve anything."

"Oh, yeah? Grandma lives in Phoenix. It would take days to get him there and while he was gone we could move across town—"

Lexi joined in the imaginary "get-rid-of-Egg"

scenario. "You could also change your name—"

"—and telephone number—"

"—so he wouldn't know where to call."

"And bribe everyone in town to keep the secret—"

"—and give double to the newspaper office to keep the story quiet—"

"And maybe by that time he'd be over this infatuation he has for Minda Hannaford."

Lexi sighed as she plunked herself down on the park bench in the small open commons across the street from the furniture store. "Minda has a knack for making people miserable—even from a distance."

Binky rolled her eyes. "Well, she's sure made me miserable. You just can't believe what a pain Egg has become ever since he got this crush on her!"

"No, I can't believe it. So tell me."

Binky shuddered. Lexi recognized her expression as the same one Binky had when she'd come down with the stomach flu. "It's his face—he's obsessed with it."

"Huh?" Lexi stretched her legs before her and let the September sunlight wash over her. "What about his face?"

Binky's eyes narrowed. "Everything. He says his skin is bad so every fifteen minutes he's running into the bathroom to wash it."

"So?"

"Then he uses my acne medication. He puts it all over himself until he looks like a connect-the-dots picture."

"I don't remember thinking Egg's skin looked bad," Lexi murmured.

"It doesn't. It looks like everybody's else's skin.

Of course," Binky mimicked, "everybody else isn't trying to please Minda Hannaford." She threw herself against the park bench. "And the whiskers!"

"What whiskers?"

"That's my point exactly. What whiskers? Egg spends the time he isn't worrying about his skin, shaving it." Binky crossed her arms over her chest and gave a loud "harumph." "My dad said he didn't shave until he was in college and that Egg is just like him. Still, Egg is all of a sudden worried about a beard. He doesn't have three whiskers to weave together to make one!"

This time Lexi burst out laughing. "Do you know how funny that sounds?"

A smile tugged at one corner of Binky's mouth. "No. Yes. I suppose. What's wrong with him?"

Lexi scuffed the toe of her shoe in the dirt. "He's in love, that's all."

"With Minda? Why didn't he pick someone normal to love? Egg is so innocent. Why does he want to hook up with the dragon lady?"

"She's not that bad," Lexi chided gently. "In a lot of ways, Minda is probably as insecure as Egg."

"But not in any ways that show," Binky pointed out. "Minda doesn't even know Egg exists and he's tearing himself up trying to impress her." Binky's eyes darted to the right and then to the left. She moved a little closer, as if a passerby on the sidewalk might overhear. "Do you know what I caught him doing?"

Lexi's eyes widened. Maybe she didn't want to know. Still, her curiosity dragged an unwilling "What?" from her.

"Talking to himself in the mirror." Binky's hands fluttered. "Actually, it was Minda he was talking to."

"Minda was in the mirror?"

"No, silly! He was just pretending she was! He was asking her out and telling her how pretty she was and telling her how much he liked her . . ." Binky made a disgusted face. "It was horrible! Really gross. How would you like to find your brother talking to himself like that?" Binky stared gloomily at her shoes. "He's going off the deep end."

Lexi laughed. "Ben talks to himself all the time."

"You know what I mean!"

Lexi put a consoling hand on Binky's arm. "Listen, Bink, just because you and I are happiest when there's a big distance between us and Minda, that doesn't mean we can decide for anyone else how to treat her. She is pretty. And she could be nice if she wanted to be. Egg has to learn for himself what Minda is about. You and I can't tell him."

Binky nodded morosely. "When you say it, it seems so sensible, but when I think about poor old Egg getting his heart broken by—"

"He'll mend," Lexi assured her friend. "I've had lots of cracks in mine and they've all healed."

Binky stared at her in admiration. "You're different from any other person I've ever met, Lexi. You're so . . ." She struggled for a word, then finished, ". . . sensible."

"Like wearing overshoes when it rains?" Lexi laughed.

This time Binky really smiled. "Thanks for listening. I feel better."

"You don't want to trade Egg in for a batch of carpet samples anymore?"

"No. I'd still rather trade him in, but I feel better about keeping him around."

Later, Lexi remembered their laughter and wished she could share it with Jennifer.

Observing Jennifer was like watching a cocoon become a butterfly—only backward.

The beautiful, laughing, shining butterfly that Jennifer had been was quickly becoming a tight, dark, closed cocoon.

Lexi heard about Jennifer's hair three class periods before she finally saw her. It was in English class, the place where all the trouble had seemed to originate, that she saw what Jennifer had done.

"Hi, Lexi." The voice was familiar but the vision was foreign.

"What have you done?" The words slipped out before Lexi had time to edit them.

She was rewarded with a tight, humorless smile. "Just a haircut, that's all."

If the shorn and sculpted locks on Jennifer's head were a haircut, Lexi vowed never to get another. The beautiful golden hair was ratted in some places and spiked in others, looking as though it had gotten caught in a fan. Jennifer's bangs were long and ragged and kept sliding over one eye. Even the abrupt, impatient movement she used to shake them from her eyes was alarming.

"Oh, yeah. And earrings." Jennifer pointed to three tiny gold hoops in her ears. "Two on one side, one on the other. Great, huh?"

"Sure, great. What's wrong with you? You look

like you belong in a street gang!"

Jennifer's eyes flickered and the hard glint returned. "Thanks." Lexi laid a gentle hand on her friend's arm. "You know what I mean, Jen." She gestured helplessly at Jennifer's head. "It's so . . . so . . ."

"I like it. All right? No matter what anyone else says. I like it." Lexi was startled to see Jennifer's eyes fill with tears. "For once I'm doing something because I want to. Not because someone else expects me to." She whisked away the dampness with the back of her hand and gave Lexi a longing glance. "Never mind. You wouldn't understand anyway." Abruptly she turned away, leaving Lexi to stare at her retreating back.

For the rest of the day Jennifer painstakingly avoided Lexi in the hallway, her head down, and mouth twisted into a grim pout.

"You look sad," Todd observed as he stopped by Lexi's locker after the final bell. "Need to talk?"

"Yeah, but I don't know what to talk about." Lexi pushed her hair from her eyes.

"You must be thinking of Jennifer," Todd concluded adroitly.

"How'd you guess?"

He chuckled. "She's been the main topic of conversation all day today."

"Why did she do it, Todd? She looks . . . scary!"

He shrugged his shoulders. "Who knows. Jennifer's always been a little . . . unpredictable."

"She didn't seem that way this summer," Lexi pointed out.

"True. It seems to happen during school." Todd shrugged again. "Maybe she's got an allergy to chalk dust that makes her crazy."

"Don't be flippant, Todd," Lexi pleaded. "She frightens me when she's like this. I don't know what's wrong with her."

Lexi's mind was still full of her friends' troubles late that night when the telephone rang.

Her father frowned as he reached to answer. "This had better not be for you, Lexi. I don't approve of your friends calling at this time of night."

Lexi closed her school books and rubbed her eyes. It was nearly midnight. *No one I know would call this late*, she thought. Then her eyes snapped open wide as her father handed her the telephone.

"Lexi, it's for you."

She reached for it hesitantly, wondering who could get by her father's irate questioning.

"Lexi, this is Mrs. Golden."

She felt her mouth go dry.

"Have you seen Jennifer tonight?"

"N—no. Isn't she home?"

The other end of the line was silent. "No. Not yet. I was just hoping that . . . maybe you girls had . . . I just can't imagine where she'd . . ."

"I'm sorry I can't help you."

"It's all right, dear. I'm sure there's a perfectly good explanation." Mrs. Golden's voice was bravely, dishonestly cheerful. "Thank you, Lexi. Good night."

As she settled the telephone into its cradle, she exchanged worried glances with her parents. Whatever Jennifer was up to, whatever possessed her to stay out so late meant no good. Lexi was sure of that.

Chapter Nine

The final rehearsal for the Homecoming skit was over and the students were drifting offstage when Todd whispered to Lexi, "Do you have time for a burger at the Hamburger Shack?"

Lexi glanced at her watch. Nine-fifteen. "A quick one. I promised my parents I'd be home at ten."

Todd nodded. "Should be plenty of time. Come on. If we hurry, we'll beat the crowd and get a booth." Despite their haste, the Shack was buzzing with activity when they arrived, and the only seats left were at the far end of the building.

"Is this all right?" Todd asked.

"Of course it is," Lexi laughed. "We don't come to the Shack to be comfortable, do we?"

"True." Todd's smile matched her own. "I wonder if the rest of the cast has arrived yet? Do you see anyone who looks familiar?"

She craned her neck and scanned the crowd. "No, not yet. I—" Lexi gave a sharp gasp. "Todd, is that who I think it is?"

Immediately, his eyes left the menu he was looking over to follow Lexi's gaze to the front door of the Hamburger Shack. There, framed in the middle archway, stood Jennifer.

At least, Lexi *thought* it was Jennifer—or a very poorly cloned double. The bizarre, nightmarish hairstyle was still in place, but now Jennifer had exchanged her usual cotton shirt and trousers for a tie-dyed T-shirt and a pair of denim jeans with a stream of silver studs running up the outside seam of each leg. Her jacket, an oversized black leather affair, hung limply from her shoulders. She'd folded the cuffs back several times in order to allow her wrists to be free of the bulky weight.

"She was in one of the skits, right?" Todd asked hopefully. "That's a costume. I'll bet that's it. It's some kind of a joke. I know Jennifer. She wouldn't wear anything like—"

He stopped mid-sentence. Todd's eyes widened perceptively and Lexi's own gaze followed his to see what he was staring at. Behind Jennifer in the entryway, another black leather shadow had appeared.

"Matt!" Lexi gasped.

"That's the guy that Minda Hannaford's so crazy about," Todd murmured. "What do you think Jennifer is trying to prove?"

"I have no idea," Lexi sighed. "But she's scaring me, Todd."

Jennifer sauntered down the aisle of the Hamburger Shack, head held high, chin thrust forward defiantly.

"Hi yourself," Todd remarked, a little rebuffed that she was acting so snooty. "Wanna join us?"

Jennifer glanced backward at Matt. "Nah, I don't

think so. Too crowded. I don't think we'll stay."

"Are you sure?" Lexi said softly. "We'd like it if you would."

Jennifer's expression faltered.

"Well, maybe for a minute if . . ." Then she straightened her shoulders again. "Looks like Matt's talking to someone anyway. Sure. Why not? Slide over. How'd practice for the Homecoming skit go?" Jennifer asked.

If Lexi closed her eyes and just listened to her voice, she could imagine that it was the old Jennifer, without the spiked hair and black leather. She stammered "F-F-Fine. Fine. It was fun. I think it's gonna be great, Jennifer. I wish you were in it."

Jennifer shook her head. "Nope, it's not for me. Those things are just dumb."

"But you did so well in the musical this summer that I thought—"

"Well, you thought wrong." Quickly, Jennifer changed the subject. "Hey! How's Ben? I haven't seen him for a while."

Lexi smiled proudly. "He's really doing well at the academy. He loves it there. He's a favorite of all the teachers. I think he's getting even more spoiled than he was at home."

Jennifer chuckled. "Good. He deserves it. He's a great little guy."

"He'd like it if you'd come to see him sometime, Jennifer," Lexi offered. "He asked me just the other day where you'd been and why you hadn't been over."

"What'd you tell him?"

Lexi dropped her head a bit, her eyes cast downward. "Well, I told him you'd been busy with school, with studying and all and that when you had time—"

"Well, that was a lie," Jennifer said sharply. "You shouldn't lie to Ben. You know as well as anyone, Lexi, I don't study."

Lexi glanced sharply at her friend. "Jennifer, don't say that. Maybe you just don't take as many books home as I do, but—"

Jennifer shrugged. "Hey, it's okay. Remember English class? But who cares about Shakespeare? He's not gonna get us a job in today's world. Shakespeare's not where it's at, Lexi. Wise up. School just isn't for everyone."

"Maybe. Maybe not."

Jennifer folded her arms over her chest. "Maybe I'll learn to repair motorcycles. I hear that's a great business."

"A motorcycle mechanic?" Todd said, his face twisting into a doubtful grin. "You're kidding, right?"

Jennifer eyed him sharply. "Why do you say that?"

Quickly Todd changed the subject. "So, what do you think about History this term? Pretty grim, huh? That list of dates, names and places that the teacher gave us yesterday, I thought I was going to go crazy—" His comments were broken off as Jennifer slammed the palms of her hands sharply against the table top.

"Well, gotta be going. Too much talk about school in this booth."

Then, much to the dismay of the pair sitting at the table, she dug deeply into the interior pocket of her jacket and pulled out a package of cigarettes.

Deftly, Jennifer shook one from the pack, tapped its tip against the table top and angled it into her mouth. From another deep pocket emerged a cigarette lighter. She lit it with a trembling hand.

Narrowing her eyes and taking a deep drag on the end of the cigarette, Jennifer pushed herself to a standing position. "Well, I'm off. It's been real, guys. Nice talkin' to you. See ya around." With that, she sauntered away, head held high, shoulders square, puffing defiantly on the cigarette in her mouth.

Todd and Lexi exchanged a horrified look. Whatever was going on with Jennifer was worse than either of them had suspected.

Homecoming weekend had arrived.

Todd and Lexi found Egg McNaughton angled forlornly against his locker as the hallway emptied on Friday evening.

"Are you going to the game, Egg?" Todd asked cheerfully, trying to draw a smile from the morose looking boy.

"No, I don't think so. There's nothing to go for."

"What do you mean?" Todd cajoled. "Cedar River's got a great team this year. How can you miss the game?"

"Yeah, well, I'll listen to it on the radio."

"She said no, huh, Egg?"

Egg's already long face lengthened even further and he snorted. "Minda? She didn't say no." He paused for along moment, then added, "She laughed in my face." He slammed his fist into the locker. "She thought it was a joke. She thought I was kidding.

She didn't even take me seriously."

"Well, you don't date much, Egg. Maybe she just thought—"

"Thought I wasn't good enough?" he questioned bitterly. "I'm sure that's what she thought. Minda Hannaford and Egg McNaughton. She just couldn't imagine it. I don't know how I ever did."

"Well, who then—?" Todd began.

"Jerry Randall," Egg said flatly.

"Jerry?" Todd echoed. Jerry had been lying pretty low since the car accident.

"Yeah," Egg said bitterly. "I suppose Minda couldn't convince that hood Matt Windsor to go to anything as tame as a Homecoming football game."

"Go with us," Lexi offered generously. "The pep rally starts in about twenty minutes. We're going to meet Binky. We really would like to have you come."

Egg's eyes glazed over with hurt and frustration. "Right. Go to the football game with my sister, just like I have every other year." He scuffed his toe on the tile floor. "What a loser."

Lexi bristled. "You're not a loser, Egg. And I certainly won't have you calling my friend Binky a loser either. Now, just quit it. Pull yourself together. The last thing that Minda needs to see is you acting defeated because she turned you down." She grabbed him by the elbow and gave him a little shake. "Come on, Egg. Show us what you're really made of. Show us that one rejection isn't going to make you give up."

Todd threw a comforting arm around Egg's shoulders. "Yeah, you know, Egg, I've known Minda a long time and whether she'll admit it or not, she likes someone with spunk."

Egg's expression brightened a little. "You think so?"

"Hey, listen, Egg. I know so. Crawling in a hole is the last way to get Minda to notice you. You gotta earn her respect."

Lexi gave a rueful little chuckle. "Listen to him, Egg. He's right. I learned that the hard way."

Egg looked from Lexi to Todd and back again. "Wel-l-l," he began, "maybe you're right."

Lexi grabbed his hand, again pulling him toward the doorway. "Of course we're right. Come on. Otherwise, we're going to be late for the pep rally."

Though the game was exciting and Cedar River squeaked out a victory in the final moments, Lexi couldn't keep her mind on the playing field. She kept scanning the crowd for a single bizarre blond head. But Jennifer was nowhere to be seen.

Making her excuses to the rest of the gang, Lexi turned down an invitation to have pizza and left. Jennifer was so much on her mind and in her heart tonight that she knew she wouldn't enjoy anything until she assured herself that her friend was all right.

The Golden house was dark except for a small, dim light in the room that Lexi knew to be Jennifer's. She rang the bell once, twice, and a third time before she heard footsteps on the stairs.

"Yeah, so what do you want—" was her greeting as Jennifer threw open the door. "Oh, Lexi, it's you. Hi. Come on in."

"Home alone?" Lexi wondered.

"Yeah. My folks went to a late movie. Some wilderness flick. Booorrring. Come on inside." Jennifer led Lexi into the kitchen and switched on the overhead light.

"You weren't at the game," Lexi announced firmly. "Why?"

Jennifer shrugged and reached into the cupboard for a large box of sugar-coated cereal and two big bowls. "Didn't feel like it, that's all." Methodically, Jennifer retrieved milk from the refrigerator and two spoons from the kitchen drawer. "Join me?" she asked, almost as an afterthought.

Lexi grinned, "Of course."

When the pair had settled down to heaping bowls of cereal and only the sound of crunching flakes had permeated the air for several minutes, Lexi began again. "I thought you loved football."

Jennifer thoughtfully stirred the milk in the bottom of her bowl. "I do. I did."

"So then why—?"

Jennifer looked up sharply. Her blue eyes blazing. "I was grounded. Okay? Is that answer enough?"

Lexi leaned back in her chair, momentarily stopped. "Grounded?"

"Yeah. Crazy, isn't it? Over one simple telephone call."

"Oh?" Lexi began warily. "What telephone call was that?"

"From the school."

Lexi's eyes widened but she remained silent.

"It seems they think that I'm an 'underachiever,' and that I'm not living up to my potential. In other words, they're saying that if I don't get to work, I might flunk out."

Lexi gasped. "Flunk out? Jennifer!"

"No big deal." But the tense lines of her face and the somber expression in her eyes said more than any flippant, uncaring words ever could. Jennifer was scared.

"So your parents grounded you?"

"Yeah. And a lot of good that's gonna do," Jennifer said roughly. She waved her hand toward the boot bench in the corner, indicating the stack of books resting there. "Like I'm gonna study or something when I'm here. What are they gonna do? Throw me in the basement and lock me in till I read the entire works of Shakespeare?" The defiant edge returned to Jennifer's voice. "They can't make me."

Lexi needed time to think. There was nothing she could say right now. Nothing to convince Jennifer that her attitude was foolhardy and dangerous. Lexi pushed away from the table. "I've gotta go, Jen. My mom and dad are expecting me home."

"What? No lecture?" Jennifer asked mockingly.

Lexi gave a small, tight smile. "No. Not tonight. I haven't gotten it all worked out yet."

"But you will, right?"

"Of course. Don't you expect it?"

They walked to the front door together and as Lexi paused, her hand on the doorknob, Jennifer asked, "Can you come over tomorrow, Lexi?" Her voice wavered a bit. "It's getting kinda . . . tough . . . around here."

"I suppose. For a little while. The parade doesn't start until one. How about ten?" Lexi asked.

"Ten's fine. See ya then and . . . thanks, Lexi."

"I didn't do anything," Lexi protested softly.

Jennifer shook her head. "Yes, you did."

"I just want you to know that you can share anything with me, Jennifer, and it's not going to change the way I feel about you."

"I wish I could believe that, Lexi. I really, really do."

"If I could think of a way I could prove it to you, I would," Lexi offered. "But for now, you're just gonna have to believe me."

The wall of reserve that had separated them shuttered into place again; but for the first time since school started, Lexi could see little chinks of light. Maybe there wasn't such a thick, tough barrier that separated them after all.

"Tomorrow?" she asked.

"Tomorrow," Jennifer nodded.

As Lexi walked away from the Golden house, she could feel Jennifer's eyes on her back all the way down the street until she disappeared from sight.

At ten o'clock, Lexi was once again at the Goldens' front door. This time, Jennifer was expecting her. "Hi. Come on in. I'm just doing some vacuuming for Mom."

"You've turned domestic?" Lexi gasped and clutched her hands over her heart. "I can't believe it!"

"Very funny," Jennifer retorted. "My dad just told me this morning that he wasn't sure I knew which end of the broom was supposed to hit the floor, so I decided to prove him wrong."

"Sounds like my dad," Lexi laughed. "Only he hasn't been around the house much lately to give me a bad time."

"Busy?" Jennifer questioned.

"Yes. His practice is really growing. He's already talking about moving into a larger building and looking for a partner."

"Great! That mean's you're here to stay."

"Hello, Lexi," Mrs. Golden said as she entered the room. "It's nice to see you."

Their exchange was interrupted by the clamor of the telephone on the hall table. Mrs. Golden reached to answer it. "Hello, Golden residence . . . Yes, this is she . . . You've what? . . . But I don't understand!"

Lexi and Jennifer both stared at Mrs. Golden, listening to the one-sided conversation and watching the deepening frown on her features. "Several checks, you say? Amounting to how much?"

"Oh-oh," Jennifer muttered and began backing toward the door. But she was too late. Mrs. Golden settled the receiver into its cradle and announced in a firm voice, "You hold it right there, young lady. You and I have to talk."

Lexi's mouth felt as dry as cotton. Instinctively, she knew she didn't want to be involved in this exchange between mother and daughter, but how to get out? It was too late.

"That was the bank on the phone. They wanted me to know that you're overdrawn on your checkbook."

"Overdrawn? How'd that happen?" Jennifer gave a casual shrug. "I must have forgotten to make a deposit. I'll just take care of that—"

"It's several checks, Jennifer. The amount is quite large." Her mother took a step toward her. "Bring me your checkbook. I want to look at it."

"My checkbook? Well, I'm not sure where I put it. I'd have to do some looking."

"Find it. Now."

Reluctantly, Jennifer slunk toward the stairs. When she returned moments later, her checkbook was in her hand.

"I don't see why—" Jennifer began.

"Because," Mrs. Golden said in a tone that was sharp and icy, "you're overdrawn by well over two hundred dollars at the bank. For a girl who rarely writes a check for over ten or fifteen dollars, that's an awfully large error."

"Two hundred dollars?" Jennifer gasped. "I didn't realize . . ."

Her mother took the checkbook from her hands and flipped to the register. "I want to see what kind of checks you've been writing . . . Jennifer, you haven't recorded a single item in here!"

Jennifer's expression drooped. "I thought I could remember it all in my head, Mom. I really did. I never dreamed that I'd be off by so much."

"You were keeping a total in your head?" Mrs. Golden echoed incredulously.

"Yeah, I'm pretty good at figures and I just thought that—"

"I'm going to have to call your father. I want him to come home right now. We have to deal with this immediately."

Lexi knew it was best to leave before the fight that was inevitable. Whispering a soft goodbye, she opened the front door and slipped out virtually unnoticed.

Chapter Ten

I don't know how to start this, Lord, because I'm not sure what it is I'm asking for. I know the Bible tells us to be specific in our prayers, and to ask you for what we need in detail, not in vague, general terms. But this time I have to be vague, Father, because it's not a prayer for me but for Jennifer.

She's hurting but she won't admit it. Hers is a silent cry for help. It's funny, you know, but that's how I think of prayers too—silent cries for help.

Like right now. I'm on my knees at the foot of my bed not saying a word, yet I know you're hearing me. I'm glad you've got good ears, Lord. Listen in on Jennifer and heal her pain, whatever it is. And if I can help—be your tool in any way, show me how. I ask it in your Son Jesus' name.

"Amen."

It startled Lexi to hear her own voice, so engrossed was she in her attitude of prayer. She scraped her long brown hair away from her face and twisted her torso until she leaned against the bed frame, one long slender leg stuck out in front of her, the other bent to accommodate her chin.

It was amazing how much someone else's troubles had taught her about prayer.

Prayer. Talking to God. One to one. Simply asking for the things you needed. It was all over in the New Testament—the part about asking.

Matthew says it in chapter seven. "Ask, and you will be given what you ask for. Seek, and you will find. Knock, and the door will be opened. . . . If you hardhearted men, sinful men, know how to give good gifts to your children, won't your Father in heaven even more certainly give good gifts to those who ask Him for them?"

It made sense. Lexi's father always wanted to help her out, give her what she needed and wanted. And he was only human. Just think of what a *heavenly* Father could do! And all He wanted was to be asked.

Jesus had said it again in the book of John. "Ask, using my name, and you will receive."

Lexi tilted her head to rest against the mattress, her eyes closed.

"Lexi? Are you all right?" Binky's voice from the doorway was quiet and edged with worry.

Lexi's eyes flickered open. "Sure. Come on in."

"What were you doing?" Binky curled into a sitting position next to Lexi.

"Praying."

"Oh." Binky's eyes grew wide and round. "You're the only person I've ever known who does that."

"Pray?" Lexi smiled. "I doubt that. Normally people just don't advertise it much."

"Maybe," Binky acquiesced doubtfully. "Do you

always have to be on the floor to pray?"

A bubble of laughter welled up in Lexi. "Of course not! It doesn't matter if you're standing or sitting or propped on your head. It's just that today, when I had some serious praying to do, it felt right to be on my knees."

"Okay," Binky said agreeably. "I hope you don't mind my asking all these questions."

"Of course not," Lexi assured her friend. "In fact . . ."

"Yes?"

"Why don't you come to church with me tomorrow. I know your family doesn't go and . . ."

Binky looked alarmed. "I'd feel out of place! I don't belong there and people would stare."

"We'll go to the early service," Lexi offered. "Usually my family goes to the late one. I've never been to the early service. I'll be a stranger too. How's that?"

"But I don't know anyone—"

"Todd's family goes to this church. And Jennifer's. Peggy's too. It'll be fine."

"You really think so?" Binky asked doubtfully. "I don't want to butt in."

Lexi laughed out loud. "You can't. It's impossible."

"I *can't?*"

"We're talking about God's family, Binky. You can be a part of it—whether you realize it or not. God's desire is for *everyone* to belong."

Binky let that bit of information sink in. Slowly she said, "Well, I suppose I could *try* it once."

"Good!" Lexi gripped Binky's hands with pleasure. "It's a good family to be a part of, Binky. Really."

A good family to be a part of—Lexi looked around the sanctuary of the church. Mrs. Waverly sat in front of her and to the left. Todd's family was in their usual place on the right, three rows from the front. Peggy and her parents were here. And there were so many she still knew only by their face and welcoming smile.

She glanced at Binky who had sat wide-eyed and still through the entire service.

"Time to go, Bink," Lexi whispered. "Come on."

Outside the church doors Lexi and Binky made a bee-line for Jennifer. Her bizarre haircut was screamingly out of place, and the expression on her face signaled that she knew it as well.

"Hi."

"Hi, yourself."

"Nice day."

"Very."

"Good sermon."

"Sure."

It was as though they were tossing a lead balloon between them and it was landing with a hard thud with each exchange of words. Binky squirmed uncomfortably at Lexi's side. It was a relief to see the pastor coming purposefully toward them.

"Alexis! Jennifer! You're the girls I've been looking for!"

"Me?" Jennifer said doubtfully. "What for?"

"I want you to help me institute a new program for our church."

Lexi brightened but Jennifer looked more dour than ever. "What kind of program?"

"Readers for the Scriptures. I'd like to have a group of high school students available who would read the day's Bible lessons aloud. I've been doing it, but I think it would be so much more meaningful for the congregation if they could hear it read from students like yourselves."

"That's a great idea!" Lexi responded. "I'd love—"

Before she could finish, Jennifer interrupted. "Thanks, but no thanks. That's not for me."

"But Jennifer—"

"No way, no chance. You can do it if you want, Lexi, but I won't."

"Jen, I—"

"Don't say anything, Lexi. I don't want to do it. I *won't* do it." With a wooden twist of her body, Jennifer stalked away.

"I didn't mean to upset her . . ." Pastor began, his bushy eyebrows knit together in concern. "Perhaps I should go and talk—"

"Why don't I do it," Lexi offered. "Jennifer and I were good friends." Lexi winced as she realized she'd said "were" good friends as if the relationship were in the past instead of the present. "I'll find out what's bothering her. I don't think it has anything to do with your new program."

"Very well. Please let me know if there is anything I can do."

"I will."

Lexi grabbed Binky by the arm. "Come on."

"Where are we going?"

"Home. I've got to think."

Binky gave a great sigh. "What do you think is happening to her?"

"I don't know. Every time it seems she might be snapping out of this . . . this . . . mood she's in, something triggers it again. I can't imagine why being asked to read in church should upset her so. I've got to figure out what's going on with her."

"Good luck," Binky responded. "I think you've got your hands full."

Two hours later, as Lexi sat scrunched into an uncomfortable ball on the front steps, she had to agree that Binky was right. She couldn't handle Jennifer alone. The longer she thought about it, the more she was sure that if she faced Jennifer by herself, it would lead nowhere. She'd prayed and as she had, she'd become convinced that a little human help would be necessary as well.

It was with a mixture of surprise and relief that she viewed Todd sauntering up the sidewalk toward her house.

"You look deep in thought," he commented as he sank down beside her.

"Did you know you were an answer to prayer?" Lexi blurted almost before his foot hit the steps.

"Me? That's hard to believe—especially if you listen to my brother Mike." Smile lines crinkled in the corners of his eyes.

"I'm serious, Todd. I've been praying about a way to help Jennifer and—here you are, walking up the street."

Todd chuckled. "You mean my idea to come and see you was divine intervention?"

"Maybe. All I know is that I have to go to talk with Jennifer this afternoon and I can't do it alone. You'll have to come with me." Then Lexi related the incident with the pastor that had occurred after church.

"So you think that you and I can go over to Goldens' and force out whatever she's keeping inside?"

"It needs to come out, Todd, whatever it is. No one can begin to help her if we can't figure out what's wrong."

"Maybe nothing is wrong. Maybe Jennifer wants to be a troublemaker."

"Do you really believe what you're saying?"

"No."

"Well, then, come on!"

Chapter Eleven

Lexi's boldness had dimmed somewhat by the time they reached the Golden house. "Maybe this isn't such a good idea," Lexi murmured in a strangled voice. "Maybe Jennifer doesn't want to talk with us."

"And maybe she does." Todd appeared very firm and take-charge. "It's time someone got to the bottom of this. Ever since I've known Jennifer she's been like two different people—easygoing in the summer and hard to understand during the school year. And it seems to get worse every year." He shook his head. "It's like she's allergic to school."

"Allergies are one thing. Spiking your hair is another."

He smiled. "Right. So let's get on with it." Before Lexi could back out, he pushed the doorbell.

It chimed inside the house, a dim, tinny clang, which finally summoned Jennifer to the door.

She was wearing old jeans and a paint spattered T-shirt. Her wild hairdo was mussed and fell haphazardly over her eyes. Barefoot and bleary-eyed,

Jennifer looked all of ten years old.

"What do you want?" she asked warily. "I'm busy." The TV droned softly in the family room.

"We need to talk," Todd announced. As he spoke, he wedged a Nike-clad tennis shoe in the door opening.

Jennifer looked from the foot pressed against the door to Todd's face and down again. "Looks like you aren't giving me much chance to say no."

"You've got that right."

Already Lexi was grateful for Todd's presence. Alone she couldn't have withstood the hostility Jennifer was radiating. Todd just ignored the dirty looks he was receiving.

"May we come in?" Lexi ventured.

"I suppose," Jennifer growled.

The two of them followed her into the family room. Again, Lexi was struck with the fact that the Goldens seemed to have electronic equipment everywhere—video recorders, tape players, loudspeakers. Not one book was in sight.

"So what do you want to talk about? The weather?" She gestured toward the windows. "Sunny and mild. No showers in the forecast. How's that?"

It was Todd who spoke first. "Snap out of it, Jennifer. This tough act isn't you. It might work with some people, but not with us."

A flicker of surprise crossed Jennifer's features. Then her eyebrows furrowed even more tightly. "I don't know what you're talking about."

Lexi leaned forward from the perch she'd taken on the couch. Much as she hated it, her voice trembled with emotion. "Jennifer, when I moved to Cedar

River, you were one of the first people I met. Do you want to know what I thought about you?"

"Not particularly," Jennifer grumbled.

"Well, I'm going to tell you anyway."

"Why doesn't *that* surprise me?"

"I thought you were funny and bright and friendly. I wanted you to be my friend. In fact, one of the reasons I wanted to join Hi-Five was so that we could be together more often."

"Really?" Jennifer asked, her blue eyes finally interested.

"Yes, really. I considered you my only friend and when you joined Hi-Five, I thought I'd lost you."

"I didn't realize I was that important." Jennifer's voice was soft and wondering.

Lexi gave a wobbly smile. "The first time I saw you, you were singing at the top of your lungs at music rehearsal. You had the music upside down and you were clowning around and seeming so relaxed and at ease—"

"Yeah, sure, 'at ease.' "

"And then we got to know each other and you *became* my friend. Remember the night Jerry Randall hit my brother with his car? You and Peggy stayed with me."

"You were having a bad night. That was nothing. I—"

"It was something wonderful! I wouldn't have made it through the night without you." Lexi touched Jennifer's arm. "It seems to me that you're living through a 'bad night' right now. It started the day school began and it's getting worse. I want to help you but I don't know how. You've got to tell me what's wrong."

"It's nothing, I . . ." Jennifer's voice quavered. Lexi moved from her seat to Jennifer's side.

"Tell us anyway."

The silence that followed filled the room with a presence so large Lexi felt as if she were suffocating.

When Jennifer finally spoke, her voice was tiny, childlike. "I don't like school. School is too hard for me."

Lexi and Todd exchanged puzzled glances but said nothing. Todd moved silently to Jennifer's other side.

"It's too hard. I get it all mixed up." Tears flowed down her cheeks and she didn't try to stop them. "So I just act as if I don't want to do the work and they call me 'rebellious.' "

"But what's the purpose, Jen? Isn't that bad? Being labeled rebellious?"

Jennifer looked up, her blue eyes were painful pinpoints of bright color in a watery sea of red. The tears ran down the side of her nose and dripped onto her chin. "I'd rather be called rebellious than dumb."

"But you aren't dumb!" Todd protested. "I've had a history class with you. You remembered things better than anyone else in the room!"

Jennifer gave an unladylike sniffle. "Fooled you too, didn't I?"

"Fooled me?"

"Sure. You know Mr. Blanchard. He never did know how to lecture."

"True, but—"

"He just reads his notes to us, Todd. All you had

to do was remember what he said."

"But you did that! I used to read for hours and still get a dozen wrong on some of those tests. How did you do it?"

Jennifer's lip gave a little twist, as if she wanted to smile. "I just listened. It's easier now than it used to be. I had to train myself."

"Train yourself?"

"To memorize everything said in class."

Lexi and Todd stared at her, baffled.

"You mean all you did was listen in class and *remember*? You could write a test from that?"

Jennifer's eyes filled again. "I didn't write tests for Blanchard. I just skipped test day. Later he'd read me the questions and I'd answer them in a make-up session. He didn't like reading test papers, so he'd let me do them orally."

"And you got *A*'s."

"Yes, but—"

" 'Yes, but' nothing! No one who is dumb can get *A*'s in history!"

Jennifer shrugged. "Maybe I'm not dumb at everything. Just reading."

Lexi and Todd stared at her.

"You know. The words."

They still looked blankly at her.

"They get all mixed up!"

"The words get mixed up? In your mind?"

"No! On the page. The words get mixed up on the page. Sixes and nines get turned around and I can't tell the letter *b* from the letter *d*." She looked from one blank, uncomprehending face to the other. "See?

You don't even understand what happens to me! I *am* dumb!"

"Are you saying you can't read?" Todd finally asked.

"Not very well. It's slow and sometimes I can't get the words to make sense." She grimaced. "That's why I've tried to take classes like home economics, speech and physical education—activity classes or anything that Blanchard teaches. I can get *A*'s in those." She shrugged nonchalantly.

"And balance out the bad grades in the other classes?"

"Something like that. If I can find books on tape, I use those. That helps a lot."

No wonder she prized her stereo equipment so highly!

"Why haven't you told someone you have trouble reading?" Todd asked matter-of-factly. "Maybe you could get a tutor."

"And have everyone know how dumb I am?" Jennifer shook her head stubbornly. "No way. I told my sixth-grade teacher that I couldn't read very well and it didn't help."

"What did she do?" Lexi asked softly.

Jennifer's face contorted with the remembered pain. "She said it was from lack of practice."

"And?"

"And she made me stand in the front of the class and read from a book."

"What happened, Jen?"

Renewed tears coursed down Jennifer's face. "I made a fool of myself. Every word seemed to take hours to figure out. I got *big* and *dig* mixed up and I thought I was reading the word *left* and it was *felt*. I really made a mess of that story."

"The boys started laughing and the girls giggled and passed notes back and forth, but the teacher wouldn't let me quit. I had to stand there, reading, until the bell rang. Then while everybody else was out at recess, I had to keep on reading." She'd turned pale at the memory and her shoulders sagged.

Todd's eyes were wide and Lexi felt a tear wind down her own cheek.

When Jennifer lifted her chin, there was a touch of defiance in the movement. "And I promised myself that no one would ever make me feel dumb again."

"So when you have a class you think you can't pass, you cause trouble?"

She nodded slightly. "Usually it means I get sent to the office to do my work. If I don't have to read out loud and it's really quiet, usually I can figure out enough words so that things make sense. It just takes a lot longer for me than anyone else. Sometimes a secretary will even read me the questions if I ask." A shadow of her toughness returned. "If I tell Mom I have a headache, she'll read out loud to me. It's worked out."

"That's why you didn't want to read in church?"

"Why shout it from the pulpit that I'm dumb?" Jennifer sighed and leaned against the couch. "Or maybe I should quit trying to hide it. Once everyone knew I was stupid, I could quit pretending."

"You aren't stupid!" Lexi protested.

"I can't read. Half the time I can't tell the difference between *saw* and *was*."

"You *can* read—you said so yourself. You're just

a slower reader than the rest of us."

"So what's the difference? If I'm slow, I can't keep up. Not keeping up means I'm dumb."

"Is it really that much easier to cause trouble in class than to struggle along?" Todd asked softly.

Jennifer wiped a hand across her eyes. "It used to be. I don't know anymore." She sounded tired.

"But the musical!" Lexi nearly shouted. "You were reading music for the musical!"

Jennifer snorted. "Fooled you. I just held it in front of my nose for Mrs. Waverly's sake. But music is easy. I always get *A*'s in school choir."

"How is music easy?" Lexi asked. The more Jennifer spoke, the more puzzled Lexi was becoming.

"I memorize it. I only need to hear it once or twice. Same with the lyrics. If I hear them sung once or twice, I can always remember."

"*Dumb* people can't do that," Lexi pointed out. "It would be impossible."

Jennifer considered the statement for a moment. "Maybe not. I don't know, I just know how dumb I *feel*." With a resigned sigh, Jennifer leaned back and put her legs on the coffee table, which was littered with tapes and records. "So now you know all about me. I'm a fake, Lexi. A liar. A *dumb* fake and liar." She closed her eyes and a single, pitiful tear squeezed from between her lids and rolled slowly to the crest of her cheek.

Todd and Lexi exchanged worried, confused glances. They both knew Jennifer was neither a fake nor a liar. But, and the question hung in the air between them, what *was* she?

Chapter Twelve

"You'd think he'd *learn*," Binky was saying petulantly. "How can a person get ridiculed time after time and still keep coming back for more?"

Lexi shook her head and said nothing. How indeed? Binky, of course, was referring to Egg's unfruitful pursuit of Minda. More prominent in her own mind was Jennifer.

Jennifer had flatly refused to talk to anyone about her problem. She'd tried that before and it had always ended in disaster. She was determined to say and do nothing. That decision left a horrible burden on Lexi's heart and mind.

"Are you listening to me at all?" Binky demanded. "You look like you're a million miles away."

"Sorry, I guess I was." Lexi brushed her hand across her eyes.

"It's okay. You're probably getting tired of hearing the saga of Minda and Egg."

"Maybe Egg should take a new tactic with Minda," Lexi suggested offhandedly.

"Like what?"

"Well, obviously chasing her doesn't work. Maybe he should ignore her."

"That would be perfect. They'd be busy ignoring each other."

"Oh, I don't know," Lexi murmured. "Minda must be pretty used to Egg hanging on her trail by now."

"And carrying her books, and washing her car."

"Exactly. That's why he should drop her."

"How can he drop what he's never had?"

"You know what I mean. He should get busy with other things—too busy to be at Minda's beck and call."

"Play hard to get?"

"That's a terrible term, but yes. Minda always likes what she doesn't have."

"Don't we all," Binky said gloomily, staring down at her well-worn shoes. "I'll talk to Egg about it. It might just work."

Lexi wished everyone's problems could be analyzed so easily. Her own life was smoothing out. The job on the paper staff was pure pleasure. It got her behind a lens and offered time to work with Todd as well. Ben was happy at the academy and had made so many friends that she and Todd were no longer his "only" best friends.

Even Jerry Randall was mellowing. Lexi had seen him planting and tending flowers in the parks as part of his public service work. He also spent many hours a week with Mike Winston at the garage. More than once she'd come upon them discussing some heavy issue under the hood of a car. Mike was no substitute for having good parents nearby, but at least Jerry had someone to talk to.

Really, it was just the problem with Jennifer that marred the peace she'd felt lately.

Saying goodbye to Binky, Lexi turned down her own street and hurried home. Her mother had said there were errands to do after school, and Lexi wanted to get them out of the way before supper.

There was a list on the table—dry cleaners, druggist, a letter to mail. Hurriedly, Lexi scooped up the list.

She'd already been to the dry cleaners and the post office when she spotted Todd's mother, Mrs. Winston, browsing in the aisles of the drugstore.

"Hello, Lexi, how are you?"

"Fine, thanks." Why did she suddenly feel so shy?

"I haven't seen you for a while."

"Busy, I guess." The urge to talk to Mrs. Winston was strong, but Lexi could think of nothing to say.

"I'm sure you are."

The inane conversation was going nowhere. Both Lexi and Mrs. Winston smiled and moved on. Then, suddenly, as if on cue, they both turned around.

"Lexi, I—"

"Mrs. Winston, I—"

They laughed awkwardly together.

"Great minds must think alike," Mrs. Winston joked. "Should I go first?"

"Please."

"I've been thinking about you all morning, Lexi, but I'm not sure why."

Lexi lowered her gaze. "I was just going to say that I felt like talking to you but didn't have anything to say."

"Well, I think that calls for a little more investigation, don't you?" Mrs. Winston said briskly. "Do you have time for a soft drink? Tea?"

That was how Lexi found herself in a tiny, cluttered tearoom near the drugstore, sitting face-to-face with Todd's mother.

Theirs was all awkward small talk until Jennifer's name came up.

"Lexi," Mrs. Winston began, "Todd has told me a little about Jennifer's behavior lately. He says she's been rebelling at school to get out of doing work that's too hard for her."

Lexi leaned forward intently. "That's it—sort of."

" 'Sort of'?"

"I really don't think the work is too hard for her; it's just that she's having trouble. She says she's a very slow reader."

"How did she get this far in school?" Mrs. Winston wondered.

"By taking classes that involved activities and speeches and other projects. She's good at those. She even gets *A*'s and *B*'s sometimes. It's just the ones that involved a lot of reading that seem to have her stumped. She can read, but she's so slow that a class with lots of reading assignments is just too much for her."

"I wonder if there's a way to help her increase her reading speed," Mrs. Winston murmured. "Surely a speed-reading class would help. I wonder if I could find out when there's a class—"

"I don't think it's her speed, Mrs. Winston," Lexi interrupted. "At least that's not all of her problem."

"Oh? What do you mean?"

"It's the words."

Mrs. Winston stared at her blankly.

"They get all mixed up. Jennifer says they get 'jumbled.'"

"How do you mean, 'jumbled'?" There was an odd note of excitement in Mrs. Winston's voice.

"Just jumbled. She can't tell a *six* from a *nine* or a *b* from a *d*. She says the words are jumbled and it takes a long time to figure out enough words in a sentence to make out the meaning. I don't really understand, but—"

Mrs. Winston stood up abruptly, gathered her purse and packages, and spoke quickly to Lexi. "I'm sorry, but there is someone I need to see. She's in her office until five-thirty and it's nearly that now. You'll have to excuse me. I'll explain more later but I really must go."

With that, she left Lexi sitting at the tiny table with a teacup still in her hand.

"Can I get you anything else?" the waitress asked, seeing that Lexi's companion had departed.

"Yes—no—I don't think so," Lexi mumbled dazedly. What had happened to Mrs. Winston? She'd hurried off so quickly that she'd left a package behind.

As she picked up the package and walked from the tearoom, Lexi puzzled over the woman's odd behavior. Still, she didn't feel disturbed by the strange way Mrs. Winston had acted. Rather, she felt an unexpected, overwhelming sense of peace. It was as if a load had been lifted from her shoulders and from her heart.

Confused but nevertheless lighthearted, Lexi made her way toward home.

Chapter Thirteen

Lexi promptly forgot the odd tea break with Mrs. Winston. Only Todd's cheerful greeting reminded her of his mother's excited exit from the tearoom.

"Hiya, Lexi. Got any good photos for me today? We're going to wrap up the next edition of the paper soon, and I wanted a couple more filler pictures for the—"

"Here's everything you need," she responded, pulling a roll of film from her backpack. "Do you have time to talk?"

"About the pictures? Sure. I have fifth period free. I'll be working on the paper, so just stop in."

She didn't have time to tell him that her questions had nothing to do with the paper before Todd was sucked into the swell of students heading for class. Thoughtfully, Lexi took her time putting away her backpack.

"Hey!"

Lexi glanced up, startled, and looked around. The hall was emptying rapidly.

"Me?" she finally asked, an unbelieving breath-lessness in her voice.

"Yeah, you." Matt Windsor uncoiled himself from the lounging position he'd taken against the wall and sauntered toward her. The fleeting thought went through her mind that if a snake had legs, this was how he might walk.

She'd never talked to Matt. She'd seen him with both Minda and Jennifer, but always felt he wore an aura of badness that alarmed her. That aura, she supposed, was what had attracted the other girls, but it only made her feel as though she were in some sort of imminent danger.

His hair was dark, almost black. It was shaved close to his head on the sides, longer on top and long-est at the back, sort of a wild, self-styled Mohawk. His eyes were as dark as his hair, a deep, muddy brown that gave no clue as to his thoughts. He was older than the other boys in their class. Rumor had it that he'd been held back a year or two.

Lexi took a step backward to her locker and waited for him to speak.

"Where is she?" he finally asked roughly.

"Who?"

"Jennifer."

"I don't know. I haven't seen her."

"We were supposed to meet here. She didn't show."

Lexi shrugged. "Maybe she's sick today." How could Jennifer get herself mixed up with this boy? And whatever did Minda see in him? Were both girls that set on self-destruction?

"You're her friend, aren't you?" Matt asked.

"Yes, I am."

"Then where is she?"

"I'm her friend, not her keeper," Lexi retorted sharply, tired of feeling scared of this boy and tired of this nonsensical conversation.

Matt grinned. "Spunky. Good. I like that."

Lexi wanted to retort sharply, but for an instant, when he'd smiled, she'd seen a wonderful brightness in his eyes. Her instant dislike for him faded a bit.

"If I see her, I'll tell her you're looking for her."

"You do that."

"Are you going to class?" Lexi wondered aloud. "We'd better hurry or we'll be late."

Matt gave her an amused stare. "Teachers expect me to be late. But you'd better hurry."

Lexi nodded briskly, relieved to be excused from the strange conversation. When she turned into her classroom, Matt was still standing at the far end of the hall.

Todd was working on the photo layout when Lexi arrived.

"I'll develop your photos tonight, Lexi. I'm sure there will be something on the roll we can use. You have a good eye for—"

"Todd, have you seen Jennifer today?"

He blinked. "No. Should I have?"

Lexi dropped her books onto the table. "Something is going on with her and I don't know what. I can just *feel* it. Like a sixth sense."

Todd laid down the paper he was holding and sat down on the table next to her. His leg dangled over the corner of the table and Lexi could see the top ribbing on his sock. "Worried?"

"Shouldn't I be? Look what Jennifer has gone and done already this year!"

He chuckled. "True, but somehow this time I don't think you have to worry."

"Then you *do* know something!"

He ran his fingers through his hair. "No. And yes."

Lexi gave him a dirty look. "And what is that supposed to mean?"

"My mother has been drilling me about Jennifer, question after question."

"Why?"

"I don't know. But I do know that my mother never does anything without a purpose. And she's got that look."

"What look?"

"*That* one. I can't explain it. Like she's up to something."

"Oh, *that* look! You get it all the time!"

This time he laughed out loud. "Come on, help me with these captions. Whatever Jennifer is doing or wherever she is, you'll find out soon enough."

"Soon enough" came three days later.

Lexi was sorting through her notebook in the English room, waiting for class to begin, when she heard Binky give a small gasp. She looked up to see Jennifer walk into the room.

At least she thought it was Jennifer.

The wild hairdo was gone. Her hair was short

now, in blond curls all over her head. Somehow, a beautician had even managed to put a touch of femininity into the once harsh hairstyle.

And the clothes. Jennifer wore a denim skirt and a soft blue sweater that made her eyes a deep azure. No more bizarre combinations, no more blue nail polish, no more fright-night appearance.

Lexi rubbed her eyes, blinked and looked again. Jennifer was walking, head held high, toward her desk. A slight smile tipped the corner of her lip and she caught Lexi's dumbfounded stare.

"After school," Jennifer mouthed. "Front door."

The day was never going to end. Lexi was sure of it. Ever since Jennifer's appearance in English class, Lexi had been unable to find her. The whole school was buzzing about Jennifer's second radical change and no one, least of all Lexi, seemed to have an explanation.

By the time the last bell rang, Lexi was so tense she felt like a spring in a clock wound too tightly. Forgetting her homework and her jacket, she raced to the front steps of the school.

Jennifer and Todd were already there.

"All right, Jennifer Golden! What is going on?" Lexi skidded to a halt in front of the pair. "Tell me *now!*"

Jennifer and Todd laughed.

"Walk me home," Jennifer suggested, "and I'll tell you what's been happening." As the threesome moved toward the sidewalk, Jennifer began. "It all started with Mrs. Winston calling my parents—"

"I *knew* my mother was up to something!" Todd

crowed and slapped his thigh. "She had *that look*."

"She asked my parents if they'd consider taking me for special testing."

"Special testing? What for?"

"Learning disabilities."

"But why?"

Jennifer stopped walking and turned toward Lexi. "Because you'd told her I got my letters all jumbled up."

"So? That's what you'd said to me."

Jennifer nodded. "I'd never told anyone that before, Lexi." She looked at the ground. "I didn't want people to think I was even dumber than I already felt. I thought if I kept it a secret and worked harder, I could learn how to do things in spite of it. But this year was harder than ever before." She hung her head. "So I thought if I turned into a troublemaker, then everyone would just expect me to get lousy grades."

"So that's the reason for the haircut," Lexi murmured.

"You never told anyone?" Todd echoed.

Jennifer shook her head. "I know now that I should have. Right away your mom suspected I might have a learning disability called dyslexia—as soon as she heard about the jumbled letters."

"Dyslexia?"

"It's a condition that causes problems in learning to read and write. It means I can see the letters and numbers, but they don't register properly in my brain."

"And that's why you don't bother to keep a balance in your checkbook?"

Jennifer nodded. "It's too much work."

"But why didn't someone think of that sooner?"

Jennifer gave a small, tight smile. "I guess because I was getting decent grades in some classes and never failed anything. I worked twice as hard and listened more attentively than anyone else so I managed to get by."

"And that's why you always looked so intense in class? Because you were just listening so hard?"

She nodded again. "I've never been able to keep up taking notes so I just try to memorize it all."

"No wonder you throw up before class!" Lexi blurted.

Jennifer's head bobbed. "Nerves."

Todd's brow furrowed. "Do lots of people have this . . . dyslexia?"

"The lady who tested me said they aren't sure—because people like me try to hide the fact that they can't read very well, but they suspect there's anywhere from one to ten million kids in school that have it!"

"Millions?" Lexi gasped.

Jennifer smiled. "And do you know what else she told me? Lots of really famous people have had it—Albert Einstein, Thomas Edison, General George Patton, even a president—Woodrow Wilson!"

"I knew you weren't dumb!" Lexi said loyally. "I just knew it!"

Jennifer grinned a face-splitting grin. "That's the funny part, Lexi. The people who've been testing me say I'm just the opposite!"

"What?"

"They said that I'm smart, very smart. Otherwise

I never would have been able to keep my secret so long!" Jennifer clapped her hands together with glee. "Can you believe it? Somebody telling *me* I'm smart!"

Lexi grabbed Jennifer in a crushing hug and Todd flung his arms around both of them. The three hugged and laughed and hugged some more. Cars on the street slowed to pass them and two little boys on bicycles stopped to stare. A pedestrian even crossed the street to walk on the other side, but Todd and Lexi and Jennifer didn't care.

Suddenly Lexi burst out of the huddle, her eyes shining. "It worked! It worked!"

"What worked?"

"My prayer. I asked God to help you. And show me if there was any way I could help you." Lexi's eyes glowed with the realization. "Don't you see? He's the one who put Mrs. Winston and I together! He had a plan all along. Todd and I were the only ones who really knew about the jumbled words, and Mrs. Winston was exactly the right person to recognize your problem."

"You prayed for me?" Jennifer's voice was soft. "Even the way I was acting?"

"Of course."

"I never knew." Her eyes flickered. "Or maybe I did. Thank you."

"Don't thank me," Lexi said. "Thank Him."

"So, let's go get those sundaes!" Todd joined in.

"Maybe we should called Binky and Egg—"

"And Peggy too. They should know what's been going on with me. I've been a real jerk—"

"You sure have!"

"Do you know that I'll have to get special tutoring, but they said there's no reason that I can't be an honor student?"

"You? An honor student? I can't believe it!"

"It's going to be hard—"

"Hear that? She's complaining already! Lazy bones. You missed the most awful English quiz yesterday. It was so hard that . . ."

Thank you! You've done it again, Lord. You answered my prayer more wonderfully than I would have ever dared to hope.

Lexi linked arms with her friends as the threesome made their way down the street, unaware of the slim, dark boy who stood in a shadowed doorway, watching.

Why is Matt Windsor always on the outside looking in? Find out in Cedar River Daydreams #4, *Journey to Nowhere*.

Turn the page for a note from the author.

A Note From Judy

I'm glad you're reading *Cedar River Daydreams*! I hope I've given you something to think about as well as a story to entertain you. If you feel you have any of the problems that Lexi and her friends experience, I encourage you to talk with your parents, a pastor, or a trusted adult friend. There are many people who care about you!

Also, I enjoy hearing from my readers, so if you'd like to write, my address is:

Judy Baer
Bethany House Publishers
6820 Auto Club Road
Minneapolis, MN 55438

Please include an addressed, stamped envelope if you would like an answer. Thanks.

———

Be sure to watch for my newest *Dear Judy* . . . books at your local bookstore. These books are full of questions that you, my readers, have asked in your letters, along with my response. Just about every topic is covered—from dating and romance to friendships and parents. Hope to hear from you soon!

Dear Judy, What's It Like at Your House?
Dear Judy, Did You Ever Like a Boy
(Who Didn't Like You?)